WHITE HOT
RULERS OF THE SKY SERIES
BOOK THREE

BY
PAULA QUINN

BOOKS FROM DRAGONBLADE PUBLISHING

Knights of Honor Series by Alexa Aston
Word of Honor
Marked By Honor
Code of Honor
Journey to Honor
Heart of Honor

Legends of Love Series by Avril Borthiry
The Wishing Well
Isolated Hearts
Sentinel

The Lost Lords Series by Chasity Bowlin
The Lost Lord of Castle Black
The Vanishing of Lord Vale

By Elizabeth Ellen Carter
Captive of the Corsairs, *Heart of the Corsairs Series*
Dark Heart

Knight Everlasting Series by Cassidy Cayman
Endearing
Enchanted

Midnight Meetings Series by Gina Conkle
Meet a Rogue at Midnight, book 4

Second Chance Series by Jessica Jefferson
Second Chance Marquess

Imperial Season Series by Mary Lancaster
Vienna Waltz
Vienna Woods
Vienna Dawn

Blackhaven Brides Series by Mary Lancaster
The Wicked Baron
The Wicked Lady
The Wicked Rebel

DEDICATION

To my treasures, Dan, Sam, and Hayley. Thank you for always believing in me. It's more priceless than gold.

TABLE OF CONTENTS

Chapter One 1

Chapter Two..5

Chapter Three..10

Chapter Four...17

Chapter Five 30

Chapter Six...39

Chapter Seven..48

Chapter Eight...58

Chapter Nine 65

Chapter Ten..73

Chapter Eleven 80

Chapter Twelve 88

Chapter Thirteen 97

Chapter Fourteen...105

Chapter Fifteen 114

Chapter Sixteen..122

Chapter Seventeen...130

Chapter Eighteen 138

Chapter Nineteen 147

Chapter Twenty..154

Chapter Twenty-One..162

Chapter Twenty-Two..169

Chapter Twenty-Three...177

Epilogue 188

About the Author...192

ACKNOWLEDGEMENT

To the wonderful and gracious Kathryn Le Veque and the
Dragonblade Publishing team: You are all the most talented,
professional people I know. I loved working with you!

CHAPTER ONE

Isle of Harris, Scotland
The Twenty-first

JACOB THE WHITE flexed the sinuous muscles in his shoulders and lifted his long, leathery wings. A thread of sheer exhilaration coursed through him as he brought them back down, snapping them around his thick, armored girth. His heart sang on the wild wind that battered his scales, in the altitude that snatched his breath as he rose toward the stars. He was flying. He was finally flying.

He'd dreamed of it for so long—a deeply rooted instinct, born from the blood of his father, Padgora of the *Sixth*, to soar and rule the sky. A haunting desire that called up from the chasm and robbed the luster from every other pleasure, leaving Jacob in an endless pursuit of its equal.

He looked around at the world in all its panoramic splendor and thrilled in the wind cutting across his wide, spiky head and scaly nostrils. He'd found it. He'd found what he'd been missing. This other part of himself.

He swung his long neck back and took in the vision of his white, spike-tipped wings. He was an impressive beast. His haunches were bursting with muscle and tipped with ten eleven-inch long claws. His jaw was as wide as three buses. His fangs could snap almost anything in two. He was power in its most primal form and he felt it. He reveled in it.

With a burst of elation at finally being set free, he flapped his wings and swung his great, spaded tail and played in the clouds.

Though he'd been altered two months ago, this was his first full night as Drakkon. He basked in it; enraptured by floating mountaintops and stars that felt so close he could touch them. The power was like nothing he'd ever known and he was unprepared for the intense desires that came with this part of his heritage, like the need for a horde, a treasure to protect, a virgin or two, and the need for food.

Everything that had breath and blood flowing through it tempted him to partake.

The first sheep he devoured sickened the human part of his brain and made him question the wonder of what he was. Almost instantly, his white, gold-tipped scales began to change. His wings folded and shimmered.

He was changing in midair! Hell, he thought, plummeting naked to the earth in his human form. He tried not to panic as wind cut off his air and the cold made his meager skin numb. For a moment, he failed and watched the ground grow closer. The backpack he'd so carefully tied to his claw, filled with his clothes, credits cards, and his cell phone, flew away. He remembered what he'd been taught. Now that his blood had been changed, he simply had to want to be Drakkon to become one. It had been what he'd spent the last two months learning to resist. But now…he was Drakkon. He could fly! He wanted to fly!

His vision was the first to change. His view, a panorama of mountain and sea, clear and vivid in the dark. Simultaneously, his skin stretched and hardened into scales while his bones decreased in density and increased in size. His organs also changed. It wasn't painful, or maybe it was because he could heal himself before it hurt. He didn't care. He loved his size and strength, the power in his wings.

His heart's truest desire, one he had learned to mask since the days he first understood it, had been given to him. Flight. He pierced the clouds and soared on the wind over the ocean, forests, and mountaintops—and he knew he'd never be the same.

He was the last son born to Patrick White, or Padgora as his father was known prior to finding the legendary Phoenix Amber. The Amber held the power to change Drakkon into man, permanently. Jacob's father had used it on all Drakkon, ending their reign, so that he could rule as a man.

Because of their pure Drakkon blood, Patrick and the other Elders lived for many centuries as men, fathering generations of children who were human in all aspects, except for their ancestral Drakkon essence.

Descendants—of which Jacob was a first generation, making his desire to fly even stronger. His desire had never been about actually being Drakkon. His essence didn't come with the knowledge of what it was like to be one. He'd never missed it. He'd been born human. It was all he knew. There would never be a chance to be anything else.

Until Garion the Gold, rarest of all Drakkon, and an anomaly born of sky and earth, appeared from their dreams and nightmares and proved that the Phoenix Amber was as worthless as a rock.

Garion's essence had the power to turn any living descendant into Drakkon that could live as both man and beast. Jacob's father had wanted it. The Elders feared it and funded an organization, to which Jacob and his sister had belonged, called The Bane, a band of White descendants trained in the pursuit of killing Garion the Gold before he refilled the sky with Drakkon.

Fourteen years after killing half of Jacob's relatives with his fire, Garion used his essence to save Jacob's life.

Healed and altered, Jacob was now one of three who possessed the power to transform at will. His sister being the third.

Jacob understood the danger Drakkon presented to the world. He'd spent years in The Bane. He'd seen the carnage one Drakkon could rain down with a few blasts of fire. But killing Drakkon was against his nature and, now, so was belonging to The Bane.

The essence of a pure Gold Drakkon flowed through his veins now. The evidence of it grew more apparent with every week that passed, affecting both his forms. He was faster, stronger. His senses were growing sharper, especially his sense of smell, and he could see in the dark. Even his appearance had changed. His near white hair and scales had taken on a golden tint. He was familiar with the lore of the Elders and what powers Drakkon possessed; telepathy, inherently knowing how to speak and understand any language, even dead ones.

Drakkon could only be destroyed by gold, whether it be bullets, sword, arrow, or Garion's tail, as long as it was pure gold. No Drakkon was permitted to burn another Drakkon, and many types of self-healing were possible.

But Garion's existence changed everything they knew. His blood could do things never possible before, like alter at will and heal descendants and who knew what else? Garion didn't even know for certain because he'd managed, through extraordinary strength of will, not to change into his Drakkon form for fourteen years. He had no idea how his blood would eventually change someone. No one did.

They did know, though, that the more power Jacob gave Drakkon, the more difficult it would become to harness.

Jacob must not risk being spotted as Drakkon and if he must take to the sky, to be mindful of cell phones that could offer evidence to The Bane and to the world of his existence. The Bane didn't know he'd been turned. He needed to keep it that way. He'd even had his last name changed so he'd be harder to find.

He would be mindful of all Garion's warnings. He'd train himself and strengthen his will. Not just in the power of altering or not, but in staying out of trouble. A troublesome Drakkon would be a dangerous thing. He understood that. But he had to fly. He could no longer pretend to have found fulfillment in being the lead guitarist of a Billboard-topping band, or in chasing women, and especially not in service to The Bane. It was time for a new path.

CHAPTER TWO

CLOUDS ROLLED LOW across the slate gray sky, piercing the mountaintops and casting the icy bays in ominous dimness. To the east, white-tailed eagles screeched above Loch Seaforth and flapped their wings above the waves, hoping to catch a fish.

The bracing wind of early spring blew across River Wray's hooded parka, sweeping it from her shoulders twice already and she hadn't even passed the next village. She gave up trying to keep her hair tucked inside and gave her ear to the sounds of nature around her. She spread her gaze over the snow-dusted mountain range around her and Clisham mountain to the west, highest in the Outer Hebrides, her nemesis. She saw it every morning on her way to work, and each day she thought about conquering it. Climbing it wasn't the issue. She'd climbed it before. Her dream was to fly beyond it, beyond all the mountains, to escape the confines of her life and her past. But she was afraid to go, afraid to face the multitude when just a few had such power over her. Maraig, as small as it was, was home. It was safe.

Part of her hated herself for clinging to what she knew, even though what she knew hadn't been pleasant. She made up for her fearfulness in other ways, like standing up to bullies and never giving up on her dreams. She'd work tirelessly at it, as long as she had to and she'd take care of her family while she did it. But one day, she'd leave and it would be her music that propelled her.

She'd known from an early age that she was sensitive to the brutal grandeur of nature, moved to tears by the otherwise ordinary. She heard music in the mundane and when she was eleven, she composed her first piece. One day, her work would be picked up by someone big and then she would have no more excuses not to leave Harris.

There was nothing here for her but memories she couldn't escape. As far as her love life went, it didn't. She wasn't interested in dating the same boys she used to beat up for teasing her. She'd been taller than most of them. Being long-legged and lanky had made her awkward. Her ginger hair, when almost everyone else's was blonde, or dark like her sister's, made her stand out. Her mother had abandoned them when River and Ivy were eight. Everyone in her village and the neighboring villages knew that Lena Wray had run off with her lover. That was when the teasing had truly begun. Most of the time, River had been so busy consoling her sister and cooking for her father that she didn't have time to fight. Most times, she did fight though—and won. And then, of course, there was the fact that her father was the village lunatic, who claimed to have seen a dragon kill a man over twenty years ago.

Her childhood had made her self-conscious as a teen.

Over the years, she'd learned to ignore the whispers about her father. Her mother...well, that took more time from which to heal.

She'd grown into her six-foot frame, becoming more confident, even leaving Harris for two years to study at Edinburgh University and testing her wings a little. She'd met men, went to bed with one of them. She thought she loved him, but when she had to leave and return to Harris, she never heard from him again. After that, she stopped looking and went to work at the shop, composing her music at night.

She didn't care if she was twenty-one, single, and living at home with her father and her fraternal twin sister. Despite the monotony of being in the same small place, with the same people, making the same choices every day, her life now was good. She didn't mind living in a mostly harsh climate, in mostly barren land, surrounded by mountain ranges, forests, and water.

She dreamed of more though. She—

She blinked her eyes on the snow-carpeted crag ahead. She stopped, and so had the wind. Did she just see a slight movement against the wall? Something gigantic and as white as the late frost? A trick of her eyes? The shadowy sky? It had to be. It had looked as if a whole portion of the ridge had inched to the left.

She waited a moment in the stillness of the morning. Watching, listening. When she was sure there was no more sign of movement, she continued on. It was nothing more than her overactive imagination. It helped when she was composing her music, but not when she was alone. Many worked in Tarbert but they traveled by road. She always chose the more scenic route, the footpath less traveled.

She'd never felt as if she were in danger until this moment. She couldn't put her finger on it, but it was as if something in the air had changed. It set off an alarm from someplace primal within her. Her flesh prickled beneath her parka. She looked toward the loch to get her thoughts off it. The birds were gone. Her gaze flicked back to the crag. It didn't move again. She was going to have to pass it to get to work—just as she'd passed it hundreds of times before.

This time felt different. This time, her hair crept away from her skin and her heart felt racy. She tried to think of other things as she grew closer, like the two years she'd spent at University studying music, and Colin…no, thinking of him and how easily he'd forgotten her would only make her feel worse.

She kept her eyes straight ahead. She could see the road to Tarbert up ahead and quickened her pace. She wasn't one to frighten easily when it had to do with anything but actually leaving Harris. She was used to her imagination taking off now and then, making her blood rush through her and her heart pound. In fact, part of her wished it happened more often.

She heard a sound like the wind blowing off the crag. Her heart thumped and, again, she stopped. She turned. She had no idea what she expected to see, but it wasn't the outline of something that seemed out of place along the ridge. She squinted her eyes. The shape blended in perfectly with the snow but shadows fell on it in a way that made it look as if it were separate from the rock.

What was it? She took a step toward it, curiosity prompting her forward. Was…it…moving, rising and falling slowly, deeply? Her heart almost failed her when she realized it was breathing! She didn't have time to doubt her observation or her sanity when a whole section of the crag shifted and what had been an outline a minute before, came to three-dimensional life before her, uncurling its huge, spiked head from its powerful, spaded tail.

This isn't real. River told herself over and over while snow, shaken from its place by the thing's movement, drifted down on her. She wanted to run, to scream. In fact, she was screaming—in her head. She was too stunned and terrified to use her vocal chords except to expel tight, little cries she tried for some foolish reason to muffle with her mittens.

Heavily-armored in pearly white scales, it rose up high above her on its gigantic legs. Arms, slightly smaller, and long, white talons clawing the air. It turned its spiked head and aimed its debilitating lapis gaze straight at her.

She didn't move, didn't breathe as she stared into its chillingly beautiful eyes. It had a wide, angular snout and scaly nostrils that blew out a gust of warm air, pushing her hood back from her head.

Dear God, help her. She tried to cling to consciousness. It was a dragon. Her mind couldn't take it in for a minute. It was a real dragon. Her father had been right. He'd spoken many times, in fact, *too* many times, of a great blue-green-colored beast flying across the sun, blackening the land and flying into someone's penthouse window. No one believed him and he'd lost much because of it.

Drawn to the magical, River had always wanted to believe dragons existed. Now, she did. Dragons were real, and big, and very danger-ous, living in obscurity among humans.

The fantasy had just gone dark.

She wanted to faint so that when it killed her, she wouldn't feel its long fangs ripping through her. It was enormous, with tear-shaped scales and...her knees nearly buckled beneath her...giant, leathery wings that stretched out over twenty-five feet.

But since she didn't faint, she decided to try to save her life—and the lives of others. Dragons breathed fire, didn't they? It could kill Ivy, her father, the people from the village. Who could fight this thing if it flew off to any of the villages? They wouldn't even know it was there until it was too late. She would have walked right by it. Her heart thumped so hard it made her feel sick.

Obscurity was its weapon.

"Wait!" She held up her hands. "Don't eat me!"

It looked at her as if it understood what she was saying, as if there was intelligence behind its piercing gaze.

"I'll...I'll make a deal with you," she managed, thinking she should close her eyes to help her stay conscious. Looking at it sapped the breath from her lungs. "Don't eat me or go to the villages and I promise I won't say a word about your existence."

What was she doing? It didn't understand her and, even if it did, her end of the bargain didn't hold much weight. She wouldn't say a word if she was in its belly.

The beast stretched its neck toward her, binging its jaws close, enveloping her in its breath. She finally closed her eyes, fighting back a scream, waiting for the pain.

I don't eat people.

His voice, husky and male, resonated through her head and rumbled through her blood, her bones, dominating every other thought. Her eyes shot open. Was that...his voice in her head? How? How was she hearing him? She covered her ears with her mittens and finally fainted.

Just before she lost consciousness, she would have sworn the dragon licked its chops.

CHAPTER THREE

THE DRAKKON WATCHED the girl crumble to the ground. He lowered his spiky head to her body and sniffed. She smelled like a flower he remembered tasting as a human and…cattle. She wasn't a virgin but there was something in her wide, luminous gaze besides terror, something filled with wonder and a thrill of excitement that made him wish she would wake up. He thought about tasting her. Just a lick. He was Drakkon and, though newly risen, he possessed all the desires of such a beast. He wouldn't eat her though. There was still enough man in him to quell *that* desire.

Man. The thought trickled across his mind and changed him into one almost instantly.

He exhaled a breath he felt like he'd been holding for hours. With it, he shed his scales, his wings, his fire. He stood naked over her now, a man in body and mind. A thread of disappointment settled over him. Just for an instant, and then it was gone. How had he let this happen? He'd let someone see him. What should he do? Get dressed. He was freezing his ass off. He looked to the side of the wall and his backpack and hurried to it.

He'd flown.

And he'd been seen. What the hell should he do now?

Sobering, he turned back to the girl and hurried into his jeans, socks, and Ferragamo boots. Who was she? What was she doing out here alone in the middle of nowhere? His teeth clinked together while he pulled a sweater from his pack and put it on. Why the hell hadn't he chosen someplace warmer?

He thought people didn't live here. He'd chosen this island to land because of its isolation. So much for that.

She stirred and he tossed on his coat and took off running around the crag.

He hid from her sight while she awakened, but he didn't leave. He watched her sit up and look around. Her hood had fallen back spilling lush, russet hair over her wide, terrified eyes.

It had been hard to hold his control when he'd opened his scaly lids and seen her, heard the cries of disbelief and terror in her head. He'd almost transformed then and there. It had taken everything he had to hold on. It was bad enough that she'd seen him as Drakkon. He couldn't let her see who he was as a man without probably destroying his life if she recognized him from the band or she found him on the internet. He'd waited, fighting the urge to turn with every fiber of his being, watching her while she stared up at him, battling her fear.

He knew how she felt seeing Drakkon for the first time. He'd been eleven the first time he'd seen one. It made him doubt his senses, for a moment, his sanity. If it hadn't breathed fire in the air and killed over forty of Jacob's relatives, he would have grown up convinced that the terrifying, beautiful beast hadn't been real. But it was, and it was married to his sister.

The girl stood up and backed away a few steps. He expected her to turn and run, probably back to her friends and family with her tale of a sleeping, white dragon. But he remembered something she had said about a deal. She wouldn't tell anyone about him if he didn't eat her.

A deal with a dragon. What kind of courage did this woman possess?

She didn't run. His heart began to race. Would she look around the crag and find him? If he turned again now, he'd lose half his clothes and validate her worst fears. Why wasn't she running away? Why was she staring at the rocks as if the dragon were still there?

"Hello?" she called out with trepidation in her voice.

Really? She was really calling him back? He couldn't help the smile curling his lips. She'd battled her fear and come out the victor. He knew what those kinds of fights were like and how difficult they were to win. He was tempted to reveal himself. But she wasn't expecting a man—and not being one was too dangerous.

Too bad. Besides having more backbone than anyone he'd ever known, except maybe his sister, she was pretty, with eyes like vast sea blue oceans and long legs in her tight-fitting jeans. Another time, perhaps, after he'd learned to control the Drakkon and teach it as it grew stronger, not to eat people.

He turned away from her finally, pulled on his woolen cap and set off down the other side of the crag. This wasn't a good time in his life for a relationship, no matter how short it might be.

Everything had changed.

Staying hidden shouldn't have been a problem.

What kind of bad Drakkon luck was it that the part of the world he'd chosen wasn't so uninhabited after all?

Who was the woman who looked him straight in the eye, unsettling his Drakkon guts? As much as he tried to put her out of his thoughts, the memory of looking into her eyes stayed with him on the way to Tarbert, the island's main settlement, and the only place to catch a ferry off Harris.

He had much bigger things to consider—like his wings. He thought of them on his walk, letting them replace the memory of eyes the color of the sea...or was it the sky?

The sky. He looked up at the rolling clouds and fought the urge to transform and splash through them.

According to Drakkon lore, Jacob's brood of Whites had once been considered "peace-keepers". Jacob had spent many of his formative years and some of his recent ones, as well, proving the whole "peace-keeping" theology was bullshit. A man chose who he wanted to be and Jacob had chosen to cause trouble. He'd been hauled off from boarding school when he was thirteen and spent the next two years in juvenile detention facilities across the U.K. Things hadn't been much better when he got out. Four months later, he got caught in a stolen car and went back for fifteen more months. After that and a vow to his sister, Helena, that he would never do anything illegal again, he kept his word and did a few modeling jobs and then formed his band. But he had already grown tired of the drugs and partying lifestyle. He'd made enough money to retire but what would he do with his days? Hunt Drakkon?

After walking for about an hour, crossing a bridge over the Adhainn Mharaig, and descending toward another loch, the fragrance of fresh air grew tainted with the scents of a distillery, car exhaust, and steam engines. He entered Tarbert and made his way to the ferry terminal to book his way to Uig in Skye. He'd hang there in the mountains for a week or two and practice until the snows melted. It was the perfect place to blend in with the snow and mist. After that, he'd make his way home to New York and plan a new course for his life.

He had an hour to kill before the next ferry left and was thinking about visiting the distillery when he saw the Harris Tweed Shop up the road and decided to go in. He could use a warm scarf. Being in Fiji made him forget how cold it could get everywhere else. Currently, ten degrees Celsius felt like ten below. The shop was small in comparison to the ones on the mainland and in England, but surprisingly large inside, with long rows of tweed bags and women's purses, coats, vests, kilts, scarves, and much more.

An older woman sitting behind a small counter smiled at him as he looked around. The door opened again. Jacob tuned from his examination of a soft scarf in different shades of blue.

"Morning, Margery," a girl in her early twenties called out and came inside. She swept her hood off her head to reveal dyed blue hair that was short on one side of her head and longer on the other. "Where's River?" Without waiting for an answer, she spread her dark blue eyes over the shop. When she saw Jacob, she went still and blinked.

Jacob smiled. He didn't need the blood of Drakkon running in his veins to know he turned heads and stopped hearts. He was crafted in long, lean muscle beneath alabaster skin and a mane of silky, shoulder-length hair. He didn't need the power of telepathy to draw someone's attention. The striking blue of his eyes, his full, pouty lower lip and strong, angular jaw served the purpose well enough. He knew how to use it all to his advantage, but he didn't now. He wasn't sure why.

"You a tourist?" she asked through red lips. "I haven't seen you around here before."

"Yes, I'm in from New York," he told her.

"You don't sound like you're from America," she said, giving him a more thorough looking over. She didn't trust him. He imagined that in small towns like this one, the locals didn't trust many.

"I was born and raised in Scotland," he supplied and returned to the scarves.

She didn't speak to him again but turned back to Margery. "So, where's River?"

"She hasn't come in yet," Margery told her.

"She hasn't?" The blue-haired girl sounded concerned and slid her gaze back to Jacob at the same time he looked at her. "She left home before me."

Just then, the door opened yet again. This time, when Jacob looked at it, he forgot the scarves...and everything else. It was her—the girl from Maraig. What were the chances of coming inside this shop and seeing her again? They had traveled different paths to the same place. Twice now.

"What kept you, River?" The girl slapped her palm on her thigh and then went to her. Jacob turned his back on them, wanting to remain unnoticed for a little while longer. "You're never late. You look upset. What's wrong?"

"Nothing's wrong. I...I saw..."

Jacob closed his eyes waiting for her to tell her friends about seeing a dragon. Should he get in touch with Garion? What would they do? He sure as hell wasn't going to hurt anyone.

"...someone from University," he heard her say. "An old friend."

He breathed with a sigh of relief. She wouldn't tell. He couldn't stay.

He wanted to look at her. He wanted to probe her thoughts, a benefit of his alteration, and hear what she was thinking. Who was this

River who'd girded up her courage to strike a deal with a dragon? Who'd dared to beckon the beast back? He wanted to know more about her.

"What are you doing here, Ivy?" River asked, sweeping past him and pulling off her parka. "Why aren't you at work?"

The aroma of vanilla and the faintest traces of cattle and chicken washed over him, making him a bit hungry again. He turned to watch her enter a small room. His gaze dipped to her narrow waist and full hips in her snug jeans, up her back to her russet mane catching light from a small window and illuminating her in shades of amber and deep orange. She hung up her coat and turned to leave the room.

I heard its voice in my head. No one will ever believe me.

Probing her thoughts, Jacob hoped she was right.

When she saw him, she stopped moving. He was momentarily captivated by the way light radiated from her eyes as they grew even wider.

"I didn't see you there." Her gaze fell to his near-white hair peeking from beneath his hat. *I didn't see it against the snow. Are there more of them out there, camouflaged against mountains and valleys?*

Jacob listened in with a heavy heart. He'd changed this girl's life today. Would she try to forget what she'd seen? Or would she become obsessed with it, the way some others had after sighting Garion in the sky? Most of the world didn't believe dragons were real. River had seen one up close and lived to tell about it. Would she?

"Do you need help?" she asked, stepping closer.

She was tall, her gaze, just inches beneath his. She was even more beautiful up close. Vastly different from the made-up and highlighted women he knew. Absent of color except for that of the wind on her cheeks and the beauty of her eyes painted in the colors of the winter sky and summer sea, her face was a compelling blend of beauty in its plainest, most genuine form. Her smile was filled with grace, her gaze filled with strength and longing.

Longing for what? he wondered, understanding the emptiness it left. He understood all too well. He could probe deeper, but it was too big of an intrusion. He hadn't needed to be taught that his new power of telepathy had its moral limits. Besides, why was he trying to involve himself in her thoughts or her life? He'd had enough unsatisfying encounters to know he didn't want any more or need any more.

"No," he told her. "I've found what I needed." Flight, fire, freedom.

She moved past him, then paused and turned back. "Have we met before?"

Did she recognize the fire in his eyes? What if he told her the truth? What if he told her he was the dragon she'd seen?

He smiled, though these, the first sacrifices for becoming a near immortal Drakkon were bitter ones.

He could never tell anyone.

Any woman he ever loved would die before he did.

"No," he said, setting down the scarf. He shouldn't stay another moment. "No, we haven't."

CHAPTER FOUR

J ACOB DIDN'T LOOK back as he made the trek to the terminal and certain facts settled over him. He no longer knew his own body. Even his thoughts felt alien. Why did this girl, River, entrance him? Why was he suddenly concerned about getting to know a woman? He never had been before. Women were a pastime, an enjoyable way to get from one day to the next. Nothing more. Was it only because, now, he would outlive every human being he knew? Was he trying to pitifully cling to some human need for companionship? In that case, what good would a human woman do him? She'd grow old and die and he'd go on living. Alone again.

He looked at his watch. Fifteen more minutes. He sat on one of the benches and waited, looking out over the loch. The sooner he got out of here, the better. He had training to do.

Dragon!

He sat upright and looked around. He was alone. The voice was in his head.

Are you there?

It was River, coming through loud and strong. He hadn't severed the probe. Hell, she was brave.

I know you can hear me. I know that was you in my head when you told me you don't eat people. Was it true?

He shouldn't answer her. He should let her begin to believe he wasn't real. But a part of him didn't want her to. He also didn't want her to live out her life in fear of knowing he was real and might return to eat her.

Yes, it's true. He changed his voice in her head so she didn't recognize it from the shop.

She didn't answer for so long that he probed a little deeper. He heard nothing. Had she fainted? He stood up and thought about going back to the shop to check, then sat down again when he finally heard her voice, soft, shaky, hesitant.

Where are you?

Far away, he told her. *But I will return if you tell anyone about me, as is our deal, no?*

Well, you never agreed, she challenged.

I'm agreeing now.

I won't tell anyone, she promised on the softest breath.

Then I won't come back.

He spotted the ferryman making his way to the boat. Finally. He rose to his feet.

Is this real? Am I sick? Mad? Am I really having a conversation with a dragon? You can't be real.

He paused his steps and looked back. *Would you rather be mad, or forced to keep a secret of this magnitude?* He was curious about her answer since he had a secret of the same size to keep.

I would rather keep the secret, she told him, her voice going a tad whimsical. *It will fill my nights with music.*

He smiled and he didn't know why. He should severe their connection. Her voice in his head was too intimate, too close. What the hell was she doing communicating with him? How could she not be scared out of her damned mind that someone was in her head with her? No, not someone. Something. Maybe she *was* mad. Seeing a dragon up close was bad enough. Communicating with it telepathically should have shaken her.

Why aren't you afraid of me?

I am, she answered. *But how often does a girl get to speak to a dragon? Besides, I'm not even sure this is real.*

Neither was he. How was it that talking to her was so pleasurable he almost didn't want to go to Skye? He was the mad one! After months of waiting, he was finally flying—or he would be once he left Harris.

Did he want to take her to bed more than he wanted to soar the skies? He shook his head at himself and turned toward the long pier. He finally severed his probe and boarded the ferry.

THE MOUNTAIN RANGES of Skye proved to be more hazardous to flying than he realized, with a hiker or two on every slope. He finally found a small vale called Camasunary, surrounded by mountains to the north, a loch to the west, and cliffs to the south. There was even a small bothy for travelers to rest. He hadn't seen any travelers for two days. It was perfect. Finally, in the moments when night turned to dawn and the desire to fly was strongest, Jacob stepped naked out of the bothy and watched the stars begin to disappear. He knew why the blue hour was hardest to resist. The stars were calling him to follow. He wanted to go, every part of him ached to go. Home. The fulfillment of his most haunting desire.

He stretched his leathery wings, the span of which measured twenty-seven feet, and caught the wind beneath them. He'd have to be quick to catch the stars. He flapped his wings and spiraled upward, piercing the light, drawn by the music of the heavens.

He broke through space and smiled at the stars before diving back to earth.

Exhilarated by his power, he soared over the water to the island of Soay, population of one. He practiced that night and for the next month. Training in isolation, strengthening his will not to change during the blue hour, that time just before the sun begins to rise and the stars disappear, and how not to become human while he was flying.

He cooked and ate his own meals and answered to no one. There was a weak signal here but he was able to reach the band and let them know he was leaving for a while. He wasn't sure he'd go back. There was nothing left for him there. Besides, the surviving Elders were likely hunting for Helena and Garion. If they found Jacob, they'd keep watch over him and he'd never be able to turn. He didn't care about playing guitar. He'd found his true passion and would find a way to live it without the threat of discovery.

It was all very exciting. But as the days and nights passed, Jacob began to feel that familiar prick of something indefinable, something that left him incomplete. He'd been certain flying would fill the void. How could it not be flying when it was all he'd ever wanted?

And then there was the girl he couldn't get out of his mind. Even while he flew, River haunted him. Part of his training involved resisting the desire to connect to her again, find out how she was doing. He worried about her effect on him. She was distracting and she wasn't going away.

For years, he'd had his pick of women, some beautiful enough to make him catch his breath, but none of them had taken hold of his thoughts the way River had. It worried him because he wasn't sure if his Drakkon emotions were involved and, if they were, what the hell did it mean? He'd never been attached to anyone before. Orphaned at three, he'd grown up with nurses, half-siblings who were always suspicions that he sympathized with Drakkon, and parole officers. He'd never loved anyone except his sister. Why was this happening now?

He remembered Garion's words to him one night on the island, after Jacob had returned from the bed of Vitiana, one of the neighboring island's beautiful inhabitants. *You might spend many years with different companions, but as the only other Drakkon among us, you will always be alone. I can assure you, it will be difficult to deal with.*

At the time, Jacob hadn't given it much thought. He'd been alone his whole life. Now, he wondered how long eternity really was. Now, love frightened him. Did he want to keep a secret until it became obvious to his beloved that he wasn't growing old at the same rate as she was? And then what? Watch her die?

It was all very bleak and he didn't want to think about it. But after another two weeks of her fresh, wind-blown face occupying his every thought, even dulling the thrill of flying, he knew something had to be done. But what?

River? he probed. He wanted to know what this hold she had on him was.

Dragon?

Her voice washed over him like starlight falling from the sky. He basked in the sound of it and smiled like a damned fool. *It's Drakkon actually.*

I didn't think I'd ever hear from you again.

You've been on my mind, he told her.

Really? She sounded cautious but curious. *Why?*

Damn, it that was a good question and one he didn't have an answer for. What was he supposed to tell her? That he'd finally been given his wish to rule to sky, but it was becoming as empty as everything else? Thanks to her. *I don't know why—*

How do you know my name?

He blinked, relieved by the change of topic. *I can read your thoughts. I know your name.*

Wait, she said, sounding a little taken aback. *You can read my thoughts, not just hear my voice?*

Hell, he was going to have to be more careful. What was he doing talking to her?

Can I read your thoughts? she asked.

He felt her trying to feel around inside his head and pulled back. *Not unless I let you.*

That doesn't seem very fair, she brooded. *I didn't give you permission to read my thoughts.*

All right, he said, startled at how easily he gave in. *I won't read your thoughts then. I promise. As for mine, why would you want to read them? I'm Drakkon. You'd have nightmares if you saw into my head.*

Did he just hear her chuckle?

I doubt it, she told him lightly. *You don't seem that bad. In fact, talking to you is like talking to a regular guy.*

Was that the reason she didn't fear him? Because he'd been too nice? He should share a memory or two of when the Elders had shot down his sister and he burned five of them to ashes. She needed a dose of reality about what he was capable of.

But he didn't show her. He didn't want to frighten her.

What are you doing? he asked her instead, sounding like a regular guy and cursing his will that had abandoned him yet again and so easily.

Composing some music.

She wrote music. Another coincidence?

I've been inspired by you, Drakkon.

I'm flattered.

Would you like to hear something I've been working on?

No. He was Drakkon *and* a musician. Music was his weakness. He'd been a fool to contact her. He—

She began to hum. The blend of her light, airy voice and the dark melody she created stilled his blood, his breath while making his heart soar. He tore off his jeans and t-shirt and ran from the bothy. His skin changed the instant it made contact with the warmth of the sun. His wings unfurled and lifted him from the earth. He spun and dipped and soared in the clouds around the mountaintops, dancing to the magical music in his head, as powerful as the music of the stars.

Was it possible?

That's what I have so far, she said, finishing. *What do you think?*

He closed his scaly lids and swooped toward the bothy. He'd inspired beauty and poignancy from her. Was that how she saw him?

It's extraordinary.

Thank you.

He wondered, as he landed on his two human feet, if she was blushing.

You sound different, she said in the next instant.

Her ears were sharp. He'd been Drakkon. She had no idea she was talking to anything else. *I was flying.*

Oh. She expelled a slightly wistful sigh. *What's it like?*

It's like...like your music, he told her, not knowing any better way to describe it. *It's soul-shaking and makes my heart sing like the stars.*

Her breath went still, and then he heard it, softer than a whisper, closer than his skin. *The stars...sing?*

He wanted to share this with her. Being Drakkon was new for him and he wanted to tell someone besides Helena and Garion, who already knew, what it was like. He'd probably never get the chance to tell anyone else.

Yes, River, they do. They sing to the Creator and I hear them when I fly.

What does it sound like?

He thought of ways to explain it in terms she could understand. *Like bells in the wind, like the weighty, broad timbre of a double bass. Like most musical instruments, stars aren't solid all the way to their core. Their sounds, or songs, get caught inside their outer layers and oscillate around inside. When a Drakkon takes flight, the sound resonates through space. Every star has a different pitch and they all come together in the heavens in a harmonic hum that reverberates to my soul.*

She laughed softly in his head and filled his thoughts with images of her in his arms, in his bed when he woke up, laughing with him while they flew—no. She would never fly.

Now I feel silly for singing my song to you. After hearing music from the stars, mine must have sounded as bad as my old guitar.

That was the problem. Her music was even more soul stirring than the stars.

River, I don't think we should continue communicating.

Why not?

Why not? He could think of a hundred reasons, mainly that he thought too much about going back to Harris to see her and get to know her better as Jacob. It was the last thing he should have been preoccupied with. And what the hell had happened to his strength of will he'd been building for almost two months? He'd heard her music and exploded into a Drakkon. The pull was so strong he doubted anything could have stopped him.

He should ask Garion about this. But then he'd have to admit that he'd been seen and was continuing to communicate with the human.

What did it mean? He'd not only heard music before, he *played* it. Why did hers move him so?

Just as when he was eleven, the course of his life had changed. This time, he wouldn't screw it up. He had to leave the band and find something else to do with his life. He had plenty of time to train in any occupation. All the time in the world.

Time she didn't have.

Goodbye, River.

Or did she?

He wanted to ask her what her full name was. What if her name was written in the Elder Scrolls, the list of every Drakkon descendant who ever lived? Garion could turn her.

No, what was he thinking? The world wasn't ready for the return of Drakkon. Thanks to Jacob's father using the Phoenix Amber to turn every Drakkon until only one remained, mankind had forgotten Drakkon and tales of them became nothing more than fantasy. Up until a few months ago the Elders weren't certain Garion existed. Now they knew. They knew about Garion turning Helena, but not Jacob. If Garion started filling the sky with Drakkon, they'd all be hunted.

Goodbye, Drakkon, she answered softly, reluctantly, and filling him with regret.

They were both mad. This wasn't some fairytale novel where the heroine rides off into the sunset on the back of her dragon. This was reality. Where the dragon might eventually eat her and would definitely outlive her.

He was better off not knowing her. He would forget her. He'd forgotten many.

EVENTUALLY, HE RETURNED to England to get all his affairs in order. He had a dozen messages from Aldric, an Elder of the *Eleventh*. He didn't listen to any of them and blocked the number on the phone. He booked a flight to go home to New York next month and took up skydiving. For now, it was the closest he could come to flying. He walked among the masses, feeling out of place in the world and in his own body. He dined alone, drawing away from the crowds...and his fans when they spotted him.

Through it all, River haunted him. Each day, the struggle to stay away from her became more difficult. He found himself glancing at women, comparing them to her. Each one came up short. He missed her voice saturating him like his own breath. He did his best to ignore the strange effect she had on him. But he finally succumbed and found himself spying on her dreams. He watched her battle a horde of spiders wearing tweed vests and caps. It was quite entertaining. He sensed her music, different from what she'd hummed for him, but no less haunting. He smiled while she climbed a mountain, danced with the stars, and then with a man.

A man who wasn't Jacob.

A man with hair as black as the roads on the Fiji Islands in the dead of night. Jacob wanted to burn it off with his breath. Who was he? Her lover?

Prior to a few months ago, Jacob had never had a jealous bone in his body. He'd never had a horde and was possessive over nothing. Until now.

In an effort to deny his pathetic state, he agreed to meet El Montgomery for lunch. El was Garion's foster sister and one of the most beautiful women he'd ever met. She was a descendant, born of the blood of Marrkiya of the *Eleventh,* and like Jacob, her greatest desire in life was to rule the sky. It had caused problems for Garion, who refused to alter her unless absolutely necessary—and problems for Jacob, whom her brother had altered.

Jacob had found El and her disinterest in him intriguing when they'd first met several months ago. But after her visit to the island and Garion's request to Jacob to keep his relationship with her platonic, Jacob had forgotten her.

He watched her enter the restaurant looking like she owned the place in a designer shift dress of dark pink crepe, cut to accentuate her narrow waist and her long, slender legs. El was the type of woman who turned heads and knew it, and didn't give a damn.

"I didn't think you'd accept my invitation," she said, sliding into the seat opposite him. Glossy black waves danced around her deep aqua eyes and a pleasant smile curled her pink lips. "You look like hell—and that's not easy for you. Are you okay? Is being Drakkon having its drawbacks?"

"Yeah," he murmured then flashed her a quick smile. "To both." Maybe this wasn't a good idea after all. El wasn't taking his mind off River but making him think about her even more. He didn't want to think about an eternity alone. A human lifetime was long enough. "So what's this about? I was surprised to hear from you."

She shrugged her delicate shoulders and glanced at the waiter when he arrived. "Guinness for me." She slanted her wide cerulean gaze to Jacob. "You don't mind if I have a beer do you?"

He shook his head and ordered a ginger ale. Once altered with the blood of Drakkon, alcohol became a dangerous poison. He let her gloat in the fact that she could still get drunk and waited patiently while she dismissed the waiter and studied Jacob.

"Your hair is blonder." She let her eyes rove over the rest of his face and then shook her head as if trying to get him out of it. He wasn't in it. "Anyway, my father's made-up birthday is next month. They're having something at the castle and they wanted me to invite you. I figured I should make amends for how I treated you on the island first."

"There's no need," he told her. "I understand what you want. I also understand what Garion has given up to keep Drakkon from the sky."

"Right, because he didn't want us getting killed by The Bane. But my father says there are only a handful of Elders who give a damn about us taking back the sky. They won't fight it."

"And The Bane?"

She waved her hand in front of her as if shooing a fly. "We can take care of what's left of them if they come calling."

"Garion won't do it," he insisted in his usually quiet voice, unfazed by her argument.

"I won't give up."

"I'd expect nothing less," he answered with a grin. "But you realize that your father gave up his essence to someday die with your mother. Nice for them. Bad for you. What if Garion turns you and you don't turn? Will you accept that?"

"That won't happen," she argued. "My father gave up his essence but he can still smell my mother on the barest breeze. They still communicate telepathically. Did you know that? He still thinks he should be revered. Honestly, he hasn't changed much. There's still Drakkon essence in him. Even a trace passed on to me is enough."

She was so determined, he couldn't argue. He didn't want to. He had no doubt she'd one day convince her brother to alter her. Maybe they'd get together one day when he was tired of being alone and she was immortal. But he doubted it. He felt nothing more than platonic affection for her.

She sighed, going back to looking at him. "You seem different. Has being Drakkon changed you?"

No. It was something else. A woman who'd crawled under his skin and into his thoughts, who tempted him, even now, to probe her mind and talk to her.

"It's a woman!" El slapped her hand on the table, still studying him. "I can't believe it!"

He looked up as she laughed. "Who said anything about a woman?"

"You haven't flirted with me once," she pointed out. "You've got this shy, uncomfortable thing going on. It's very charming, but it's not like you."

"She's just someone I met," he admitted, giving it little regard. "She's sticking in my head a bit."

"Wow," El said, sitting back and folding her hands over her chest. "She must be something. What's her...wait, she's not Drakkon."

"No," he said quietly, letting that monumental fact sink in deeper.

"Oh." El's demeanor changed and she leaned forward in her chair to cover his hand with hers on the table. "That sucks."

He waved away her sympathy. "It's okay. She'll go away."

But she didn't, and the next morning she came bursting through his thoughts like a wave, tossing him from his bed.

DRAKKON.

At first he thought he was dreaming. But then he wiped his sleepy eyes and smiled. *Good morning, River.*

She was silent for so long, he whispered her name, knowing she was still there by the sound of her breath in his head. Something was wrong. *What is it?*

I thought I could trust you, Drakkon.

Have I given you reason not to?

Yes, you have, she answered. Was she crying? Did she just sniffle? *You're a liar and a coward, and since you went back on our deal by coming back to Maraig, I'm going to tell anyone who will listen about you.*

His head was spinning. What the hell did she mean he'd gone back on their deal by going back to Maraig? *River, I haven't been anywhere near—*

You told me you were far away, yet you greeted me with "good morning". You're not even in a different time zone. Everything out of your mouth has been a lie. Now get out of my head! she shouted at him. *You're a danger and you need to be found and stopped.*

She was going to tell people about him. He'd be hunted and he hadn't even been Drakkon for a full six months. He—

Why did she think he'd returned? She couldn't have seen another Drakkon unless Garion or Helena had flown to Harris. Since they were hiding from The Bane, it couldn't be them. There was no one else.

Tell me what happened, River. Tell me or I'll never leave you thoughts.

You know what happened. You feasted on half my father's cattle and burned the rest. It was his livelihood and you robbed him of it. Not to mention what you did to the poor cattle!

Jacob's stomach dropped to his bare feet. It sounded like a Drakkon attack but it couldn't be.

It couldn't be.

And if it was, what the hell was it doing near River? He wasn't about to wait to find out.

CHAPTER FIVE

R IVER WATCHED NOAH Munroe and three of his friends clean up what was left of her cattle. They'd loaded up the half-eaten carcasses into the back of Noah's small pickup and were now shoveling up the rest.

A summer breeze wafted through the vale like dragon's breath, filling her nostrils with the stench of charred meat. Everything her father had.

I didn't do it, River.

She scowled at the dragon's voice invading her thoughts. If she heard it for the next ten centuries, it would never cease to jar her. She'd fainted the first time she'd heard it. But then she'd grown to like the husky timbre of it, the way it filled her to her core, like mist filling all her shadows, and swept her away to a place where the stars sang. But he'd gone back on his word. He'd come back and destroyed her cattle. Why hers? He'd been nice to her. She'd almost hoped they could be friends. How many people could say they were friends with a dragon?

Why, Drakkon? Why did you do it?

I didn't. I give you my word.

Then what did? she demanded. Her heart went a little cold at the thought of more of them going around undetected. *How many more of you are there?*

Apparently, there is one more than I thought, he admitted.

And when had she started referring to a dragon as *he* instead of *it?* It was a predator, an intelligent and very dangerous one for all mankind.

Where are you now? she asked him.

On my way to Tahiti.

Good. Never come back.

"That's almost everything, River," Noah called out to her, his truck loaded with the remains of her father's life. Wray cattle had provided some of the best Scotch beef in Scotland.

How would they live on her and Ivy's paychecks? She was going to have to try to get some hours in the distillery.

She waved to Noah, whose younger brother, Graham, would likely marry Ivy in the next year. The two had been friends before they could walk.

"Thank you, Noah. Stop and let me make you lunch. It's the least I can do." She was happy when he nodded and set down his shovel. She missed Noah and their talks. He'd always been her friend. He gave good advice and had always done his best to protect her from the children who'd bullied her. She wanted to tell him first about the dragon.

Who is Noah?

She closed her eyes and gritted her teeth. *I told you to leave me alone.*

What color is his hair?

What?

Why was this crazy reptile concerned with the color of Noah's hair? He'd retuned and attacked her farm, and he was taking about hair? Why was she speaking to him?

Is it black, River?

Black? Colin's hair was black.

Why? she asked. *Why do you want to know?* Did he know something about her ex from Edinburgh? How would he? He'd told her he wouldn't read her thoughts. Had he lied about that, too?

Never mind.

She waited for more but nothing came. Was that it? Was he finally going to do as she asked and leave her and her village alone? She had a feeling it wasn't over. Was he going to eat Colin? She wasn't as opposed to the idea of it as she thought she'd be.

She smiled when Noah and his friends reached her and invited them inside.

When she turned for the door after them, she spotted someone coming up the road from Tarbert and heading for Noah's pickup. Summer sunlight glinted off wheaten, shoulder-length hair tied at the back of his neck while he bent his nose to the carcasses.

"Noah," she called out to her friend inside. "Do you know this guy?"

He was tall, at least 6'2" and solidly built. He wore a leather backpack over a black leather jacket, slim black jeans and lace-up boots. Every single thing about him was appealing. She'd never seen him— no, she thought as he left the truck and came toward the house, she had seen him before. In the shop. The same day she'd seen the dragon.

She'd never forget his beautiful face, his shy smile, the cut of his strong chin and wide jaw. Or his eyes, like sapphire jewels on fire from within. Who was he? What was he doing back here? Was it a coincidence that the two times she'd seen him were on days when the dragon was around? She had no idea if it meant anything, but she wouldn't take chances.

She kept her eyes on the stranger approaching her door. A breeze blew a rogue lock of white hair tinged with the palest traces of gold across his eyes.

"Never seen him before," Noah said, stepping in front of her. "Can I help you?"

The stranger quirked his full mouth into a friendly smile, flashing straight, white teeth. River's heart skipped a beat. "Are you the owner of this farm?" he asked Noah, looking him over from foot to golden crown.

"The farm belongs to my father, Hagan Wray," River said, stepping forward.

He set his molten gaze on her and reached out his hand. "Jacob Wilder."

River let him take her hand and, for one insane moment, she couldn't feel the rest of her body, only her quickened heartbeat. His touch was warm, firm, lingering. His voice was soft and husky, his words, slow and laced with an accent she couldn't place. Scottish, with traces of American, a little German, and a whole lotta sexy. His gaze and his smile softened on her, as if he knew her and was happy to see her again, though they'd only met briefly that morning in the shop.

"I'm River Wray," she said, taking back her hand and trying to steady her breath. She'd seen handsome men before, but hell...no one like him. "What can I do for you?"

He looked to the field to their left, where the charred remains of her cattle remained. "I've come to help make certain this doesn't happen again."

"What doesn't happen again?" Noah asked him. "Do you know what happened here? Because we don't."

Mr. Wilder's gaze hardened as he returned it to Noah, but his smile remained intact. "I'm afraid I'm only at liberty to speak with Miss...?" He flicked his jewel-like gaze to her and waited for confirmation of her marital status. When she nodded, he continued. "With Miss Wray about it."

"At liberty by who?" Noah demanded. He was a big guy, a descendant of Viking blood. But Mr. Wilder's level gaze on him didn't waver.

"By the government," he answered Noah with a note of impatience in his voice.

"Which one?"

"All of them."

River's face drained of color. They knew about the dragon. What were they going to do? Did they think she was involved with it?

"Do you have I.D.?"

Mr. Wilder handed her three. They all looked very official but none of their names meant anything to her. "I'm a hunter," he said, returning his gaze to hers. "In order to catch my prey, I must remain as elusive as my enemy."

His enemy. He was here about the dragon, no doubt. He said he was a hunter. He was here to kill Drakkon. How did she feel about it? Why did the dragon have to kill her cattle?

"May I speak with you privately, Miss Wray?"

Whether he was a hunter or a loon, she had to find out what he knew, hear what he had to say. He wouldn't talk to her with Noah and the others there, so she turned to her old friend. "I'll be fine," she assured him. "Keep Ivy inside for me, will you?" It took a bit of convincing but Noah finally left her side.

Left alone with the stranger, River squinted at him in the sun. "Why are you here?"

"May we walk?"

She nodded, wondering how many of his softly spoken requests she would give in to. She followed when he led the way to the field.

"You said you were a hunter." He smelled good and he looked expensive she thought, walking at his side. "What do you hunt?"

He remained silent for a moment and then paused in his steps to look at her when he spoke. "Dragons."

She knew it but her legs still trembled beneath her. Despite seeing the dragon and speaking to him in her head, there was still a small part of her that doubted any of it was real. Jacob Wilder, whoever the hell he was, just confirmed that it was.

"I know what you must be thinking, Miss Wray. But I assure you dragons are real."

"Oh, trust me, you don't know what I'm thinking." Should she tell him she'd seen the big white one he was probably here hunting the last time she saw him? About the one her father had seen years ago? She didn't know how she should react to his statement. Her father would love the validation but there was only one thing she wanted to know. "How many are there?"

"There are a few," he said in his slow, seductive voice, as if he weren't talking about dragons but the weather.

While the thought of it scared the hell out of her, she couldn't help but rejoice that, perhaps, it wasn't Drakkon who'd done this. "Why are you telling me this?" she asked him as they entered the field. If he was with some secret agency, wouldn't this all be top secret stuff?

"Because when I was here last, I had tracked one to a crag nearby. I had just missed him, but I saw you. You've seen the dragon, so I'm not telling you anything you don't know."

River's heart pounded but she worked to slow it. He knew she'd seen the dragon. Was his agency going to kill her to keep her quiet?

"Why didn't you say something in the shop that morning?"

"There wasn't any reason to," he told her, bending to the charred grass and lifting some to his nose. "Contrary to what you think, we don't care who sees them. The testimonies that the rest of the world scoffs at usually give us our best leads. We want people to come forward, but I wasn't about to force information out of you."

That was reasonable, and a relief. He was who he said he was, a hunter of dragons hired by the world's governments. He knew a thing or two about dragons. "Do you think the dragon I saw is the same one that did this?"

He could have easily said yes. But he didn't. He didn't have to tell her anything else. But he did. "The one you saw, the White, has been peaceful for a long time," he said, standing again. "He's difficult to find because he leaves no evidence of his presence. He's careful. He doesn't go around killing and burning people or cattle. If he did, we would have known about it."

If Drakkon wasn't responsible for this, then she owed him an apology, and would keep her end of the bargain. She wouldn't tell Mr. Wilder anything.

Drakkon? She called out in her mind while Wilder looked around more. *Can you hear me? I'm sorry.* She waited, listening, but no reply came.

"So now what, Mr. Wilder?"

"Now," he drew in a deep breath. "You have another problem. One that only I can help you with."

"Thank you, but I have a question," she said, then laughed. "More like a million actually."

"Ask," he gave in on a whisper and a smile that warmed his eyes.

It was difficult to concentrate with him looking at her like he would have given anything she asked. Why would he? She was nothing special. She didn't try to look less plain with makeup. She was happy with her big "ghostly" eyes and gangly body. But a man like Jacob Wilder would never be content with someone like her.

His eyes sparked with shards of gold encrusted in sapphire she hadn't noticed before. They roved over her features, her hair, taking her in as if he'd just laid eyes on the world's greatest treasure. She was tempted to smile at him, but she was afraid she might fall into his arms like some stricken fool.

"If the 'White' as you call him, is peaceful, why were you hunting him?"

He pushed his stray hair behind his ears. "I was raised to hunt them," he answered quietly. "To believe that no matter how dormant they were, they would eventually rise. It would seem," he said, returning his sun-drenched gaze to her, "one of them has. I can't let this get any worse."

"No, you can't," she agreed, and then had a thought. "Maybe the white dragon can help us."

She was surprised that such a laid back fellow would let a simple suggestion ruffle him to the point of not being able to speak for a moment.

You think I'd aid a man who has been like a boil on my ass for the last four months?

She was even more surprised at how happy she was to hear Drakkon's voice.

"And what do you mean *us?*" Mr. Wilder asked before she could reply to Drakkon. "There is no *us*. You're not a hunter and you must never think you can fight and kill one. Do you understand? I don't know what we're dealing with here, but it's a dragon. It flies. It breathes fire. It may not stop at eating cattle. If you see it, promise me you'll hide."

River, promise the worm. He's right.

"I promise."

He smiled, looking too relieved for a man she just met. Why would he even worry that she'd try to fight a dragon? Did he think she was an idiot?

You faced me down fearlessly, Drakkon's voice echoed through her head.

Right, River agreed, *but he doesn't know that. He only knows that I saw you.*

Wilder muttered something unintelligible and then fumbled for something in his backpack. "Do you have WiFi? I need to make a call."

"No, but most of the B&Bs in Tarbert do."

He looked up at the sky and then back toward the road. "I just came from there. I should have checked."

She smiled behind her hand. "Yes." He should have. Tarbert was over an hour's walk away. "I could ask Noah to give you a ride."

"No," he said, stopping her when she moved to return to the house. "I don't mind the walk and it's important that I make the call." He didn't leave right away but shoved his hands into the front pockets of his jeans. He moved his tongue against the side of his cheek then ran it over his lips. "Are you going that way?"

She shook her head.

He raised his brows. "To work? At the Tweed shop?"

He remembered her then. She didn't know why it made her want to smile. "It's Sunday."

He thought about it for a moment and then shook his head at himself and laughed. The sound was more like a short series of deep baritone grunts that made the soles of River's feet burn. "Ah, right, it is."

Dolt.

Stop it. I think he's sweet.

And what else?

She didn't answer but blushed looking at the shape of the hunter's mouth. His bottom lip was plump and pouty and fashioned to be bitten.

His dipped his chin and smiled when he caught her admiring them. She blushed an even deeper shade of magenta.

"I'll be back soon."

"Oh? You're coming back then?" she asked twisting a belt loop of her jeans.

"Yes." He lifted his gaze to hers and let his smile shine on her full force. "I'm going to protect you."

She watched him go, wanting to laugh. Had the dragon hunter ever seen a real dragon? Did he know how big they were? Jacob Wilder didn't even carry a weapon, unless he had one hidden in his backpack. How was he going to protect her? Why her? Why not some other farmer who might be in the dragon's path? The dragon who ate her cattle was probably long gone by now. But what if it wasn't? Did Mr. Wilder know something and wasn't telling her? She looked around at the mountains and cliffs in the distance. It could be hiding anywhere.

Don't be afraid, River.

I'm not afraid, Drakkon. Mr. Wilder has promised to protect me.

He snorted—or breathed fire. She wasn't sure which. When he spoke, pure, unadulterated arrogance coated his voice. *What can a man do that Drakkon cannot?*

She looked up at the sky. What she needed was a dragon to protect her from another dragon, but Drakkon had chosen Tahiti. "He can be here, apparently," she muttered aloud and headed back to the house.

Drakkon was silent.

CHAPTER SIX

J ACOB DIDN'T WANT to leave River at the house without protection, but he had to try to get his sister and brother-in-law on the phone. Find out what, if anything, they knew of a fourth Drakkon. It was most definitely Drakkon that had attacked River's farm. Was it a coincidence that the same person would have an encounter with two different Drakkon? It didn't seem likely, and that's what worried him. What if it had burned the house instead of the field? What if it had killed her?

He was going to find it and kill it before it returned. In the meantime, he'd stay close to her. He realized that he felt overwhelmingly possessive toward River. He knew it wasn't a good thing. It showed up when he decided to fly here instead of using the ferry. The need to get to her had nearly made him forget his pack...and the fact that he was a man. *That* was jarring. He'd almost lost himself completely to Drakkon. He'd almost turned and snapped his fangs at her male friend, Noah. Thankfully, he'd controlled himself. He liked her. He liked how she smelled. That didn't make her his.

The Drakkon within disagreed.

She liked the dragon. He didn't have to read her thoughts to know it. Should he tell her the truth? That he was the White? He'd already told her too much, but he had to make his purpose there believable and spilling his guts was too tempting. The secret was already too difficult to bear alone.

He wasn't sure yet what his intentions toward River Wray were. He knew as much about matters of the heart as he did about being Drakkon. He'd never been the guy who stuck around. He'd never committed because he'd always felt incomplete. How could he give a hundred percent of himself if he wasn't whole?

He was whole now. Man. Drakkon. He was complete. At least, he'd felt complete just before he'd begun talking to River in his head, before he'd heard her music. Seeing her again didn't help. Being near her in his human form, talking to her with his mouth and hearing her with his ears only made his attraction and curiosity stronger. He smiled, thinking about her believing she wasn't anything special. He already liked her more than almost all the people he knew. She had guts. She'd made a deal with Drakkon, not just for her sake or her family's, but for her village. She'd kept her end of the bargain, loyal to her word. And she had a beautiful voice. He wanted to help her, to stay close to her, to possess her. He knew he shouldn't. She was trouble. She could steal his heart if he let her. But trouble never stopped him before.

He was willing to confirm to her—as a man who'd trained his whole life to hunt them—that Drakkon were real. She already knew it. She thought he'd attacked her farm. Pretending to be someone else was the only way to clear his name and it had worked. She no longer suspected him. She was no longer angry with him. And he cared if she was, damn it.

Why now? Why let himself develop any kind of feelings for some-one now when he had a new thrilling path to take? Why had he stayed in England instead of going home to New York? Because she would have been out of range. She wouldn't have been able to contact him.

So what if a Drakkon ate a few cows or sheep? He'd done it. But this new Drakkon had burned what it didn't consume. Who was it? *How* was it? Garion was the only way to become Drakkon. Had he recently transformed anyone? No. Never. Garion was rightly against turning the sky over to Drakkon. Both Jacob and his sister had to be knocking at death's door before he'd given in and altered them. He wouldn't have changed anyone else.

The only other Drakkon Jacob knew about was Jeremy the Red. He'd procured Garion's blood and had used it on himself. But Garion had killed him with his golden tail, the only element that could kill

Drakkon.

Something suddenly dawned on him...Garion and Helena had been shot with golden arrows and had healed themselves. Could the Red still be alive? Jacob's stomach turned at the thought and it fired his blood. Jeremy was a vengeful bastard. Had he somehow found out that Jacob had been altered? Had he picked up Jacob's scent in Harris and gone after him? Was he in Harris because of Jacob?

He quickened his pace. He wanted to turn back but Garion needed to be told that the Red was possibly alive. He couldn't use telepathy since the range was only two thousand miles. The phone would have to do.

He hurried toward Tarbert, thinking about River as he went.

You didn't tell the man about me, he sent to her. He liked being able to talk to her whenever the urge struck him. Which it did often. Now that he was here with her, he didn't need to continue using telepathy—to continue speaking with her pretending to be a Drakkon. He shouldn't. It was sneaky.

I was wrong to accuse you. I intended to keep our deal, Drakkon. But he already knew.

Jacob liked her. It was pretty big for him. In the past, he found that he stopped liking most women a few hours after meeting them. Many stopped liking him, as well. He was often distracted with thoughts of something more and it was evident in his careless treatment. But it was different with River. He liked her more each time he spoke to her. They just seemed to click and fit. But it wasn't him she sang to. In her mind, he was Drakkon.

I'll keep my end of the bargain, too.

She was quiet for a moment, then, *I wish you didn't have to. If you don't eat people then I don't see a reason to ask you not to come back.*

There it was. She liked Drakkon. And Jacob liked that she did. But he still didn't trust his Drakkon self around her. He didn't know how his instincts would react to smelling her. He'd wanted to lick her the first time he'd seen her through bigger eyes.

For now, he'd get to know her as Jacob Wilder. He didn't want to think about later.

The truth is, I don't know if I'd eat someone, say, like Noah. I haven't been around many people.

Are you jealous of Noah, Drakkon?

Not at all, he defended. *I just used him as a point of reference.* He still couldn't believe that he was, in fact, jealous and he sure as hell wasn't going to admit it to her. Jealousy was an insecurity Jacob hadn't suffered in the past.

Well, I don't like that reference, she said curtly. *Maybe it's better that you stay away.*

Who was this guy, Noah, that she would protect him? And why did it make Jacob want to eat him?

You love him then?

Yes, like a brother.

That was better to hear. Jacob smiled with relief as he entered Tarbert. *Then I'll never speak of eating him again.*

Thank you.

He hurried to the small B&B and went inside.

I just spotted a shark over the Pacific that would fill my belly 'til morning, he told her, needing time to speak to Garion. *Excuse me while I go get dinner.* He didn't worry about shocking her. She was going to have to get used to it if she wanted to be friends with Drakkon.

WiFi was only for guests, according to the owner of the B&B, Charlie Owens. So Jacob paid for a room facing the loch and sat on his bed to make his call.

The island in the South Pacific had WiFi, paid for by his millionaire brother-in-law. The connection went through and Jacob waited impatiently for Garion to pick up. He was about to hang up and call his sister's cell, when the ringing stopped.

"Jacob," Garion's voice came over the other end. "Where are you?"

"Harris, in Scotland. Where's Helena? She should hear this."

"She's here. You're on speaker."

"Jake?" his sister said. "Everything all right?"

42

"No. There's another Drakkon." He waited a moment for the stunned silence to settle over them. Then, "Have you turned anyone?"

"What? No, of course not. What the hell has happened?"

"Garion, I think it's Jeremy," Jacob told them wasting no time.

"No," Garion said, his voice the rumble of thunder. "It can't be."

"Back in Norway," Jacob reminded them, "when we fought The Bane and I killed Jarakan and the other Elders, you were both shot with gold-tipped arrows. Why didn't either one of you die?"

"Because we…" Garion paused and Jacob heard his sister swear an oath. "I *am* Gold," Garion continued, realizing what it meant. "Golden weapons have no effect on me—or anyone who shares my blood." He was silent for a moment. Jacob thought he could hear Garion's heart through the phone as a terrible truth dawned on him. "Thomas…we…we burned Thomas and he wasn't dead."

Jacob closed his eyes as the weight of it all settled over him. Jacob's brother, Hendrick, had shot down Garion's first foster father, Thomas White, along with two of Garion's childhood friends. The bodies had been burned. No one had known then the power of Garion's blood or that the altered Drakkon were not dead, just regenerating.

"I'm sorry, Garion," Jacob told him, truly heartsick for him. "But we need to find a way to kill the Red."

"Tell us what happened," Helena said when her husband remained quiet, still processing what it all meant.

Jacob told them everything they needed to know about the attack on the Wray farmstead the night before. He'd visited the scene. The land had been charred by Drakkon fire. Jacob had been in Harris two months ago and then had left.

"Yes," his brother-in-law said when he was finished. It sounded more like an answer to a question someone else had asked. Jacob guessed his sister and her husband were speaking telepathically. They'd done it often in Fiji, leaving him out of entire conversations, laughing at seemingly nothing, blushing for no reason. Right now, he guessed his sister was consoling her husband and bringing him back to the present.

"Let me get my Onyx," Garion said in the next moment.

Jacob had forgotten about the seeing stone. It could locate any Drakkon in the sky. It was just what they needed to find the Red.

"So," his sister's voice broke his reverie. "How did you say you found out about the attack?"

He hadn't said. "I heard about it."

"You weren't in Harris when it happened, right? You said you'd left. So, who did you hear it from?"

Hell, she'd always had a way of digging deep for answers in directions other people wouldn't think to go.

"El called and said she had lunch with you."

"Yeah." Here it came. El told Helena what he'd told her.

"She said you looked ragged."

"I hadn't been sleeping." He waited for more but nothing came.

"Are you okay?"

He'd like to tell her about River, ask her advice about things. But she'd figure out too soon that he'd been seen, that he had communicated with a human while he was Drakkon, and that he wanted to tell the human everything. "That's not important right now, Helena."

"Back." Garion's voice thankfully interrupted whatever his sister was going to say next. "There's no sign of him in the stone, Jake. How certain are you that this was a Drakkon attack?"

"Some cattle were bitten in half. I don't know any other creature with jaws that big and powerful, except a crocodile, and there aren't any crocs here, Garion. The rest of the cattle were charred—not set afire with torches, but charred to the bone. It was Red. He didn't die, just as we didn't die."

"Right," his brother-in-law pulled himself together and agreed. "Helena and I will be there sometime tomorrow. I'll book our flights—"

"No. No, I don't need you both here." He didn't want to tell his sister and her husband that he'd let someone see him after his first night out. He didn't want to tell them that he'd stayed in touch with her, came back to her, and didn't want to leave. "You'll rile up the villagers the second they see you."

"We're not coming as Drakkon," his sister said.

"You don't need to for these people to take notice of you. The last time I saw you, Helena, your hair was down to your ass and almost as gold as Garion's. You both stand out too much. I'll take care of Jeremy the Red."

"Don't be an idiot, Jake," his sister said impatiently. "Of course we're coming. The Red could return faster than we could reach you. He could be there now as a man. Either we go to you or you come to us. Which is it going to be?"

"Neither," Jacob insisted. "I can handle this myself."

"We're hanging up now, Jake."

Damn it, sometimes he really wanted to strangle her. "Alright. Give me a week."

"A week for what?" Helena pried.

"To calm the villagers down. They don't know what the hell attacked them. We don't want whispers spreading to the tabloids."

A long silence passed between them. So long that Jacob knew they were talking alone. "Hello?" he snapped into the phone.

"Okay," his sister snapped back. "We'll see you soon."

"Yeah. Great," he drawled. He knew their concern was warranted. They had to stop the Red and three was better than one. He couldn't believe he was actually going to hunt a Drakkon. It would be his first time, despite all his training. "Garion?" he said before they all hung up. "How are we going to kill it?"

"Last time we saw him, his arm that I had bitten off hadn't grown back. If that hasn't changed, then we cut off his head."

Not something Jacob was looking forward to doing. He was trained in killing Drakkon, not men. Cutting off a Drakkon's head was nearly impossible. There was no weapon big or powerful enough to cut through scales. Jeremy would have to be taken down as a man, and cutting off a man's head was not in Jacob's comfort zone.

Jacob clicked them off, then paused to do a little online research about Highland cattle and make a few calls. Thanks to the money the band made, his inheritance, and a few "trinkets" Garion had given him, worth over two and a half million dollars, he could afford to buy what he wanted. He'd made some investments from Fiji and still had more than enough.

Thankfully, Mr. Owens was still sitting at the front desk and was able to give Jacob the address of the post office in Tarbert.

Everything okay? He sent to River while he tossed his soon-to-be useless cell into his backpack and left the B&B.

Yes. How was the shark?

What would Garion and Helena think of him communicating with River the way he did? He didn't care enough to stop. He liked talking to her. He liked it almost as much as flying. How was it possible? Had becoming Drakkon made him mad?

It was delicious. How was your meal with Noah?

Fine. I asked him to come back tomorrow to finish clearing up the field.

Why?

Because Mr. Wilder is coming back and I don't know what questions he'll ask. I don't want Noah hearing about dragons from a dragon hunter.

You don't like Wilder, do you. It wasn't a question but a suspicion. One that didn't please Jacob. It was because of Drakkon. Why would she like a guy who was out to kill her new pet? This whole ridiculous thing could backfire on him. Did she like his Drakkon too much to like him as a man? Why did he care? He was only here to protect her and then he was flying back to Fiji—on a plane.

I don't know him enough to like or dislike him. He seems nice. He's a little awkward for a guy who looks the way he does.

Oh? How does he look?

Like he should be in the movies or on a beach in Australia.

Jacob smiled. *His appearance pleases you then?*

He knew picking her brain about him was a crappy thing to do. She thought she was speaking to someone else. It didn't put them on equal footing and he wanted to be fair. Besides, if he ever told her that he was Drakkon, the one in her head all this time finding out her every thought and desire, while pretending to get to know her as Jacob, she'd hate him. *You know what?* he interrupted before she had time to reply. *Don't answer that. I'm sleepy. I'm going to find a place to rest.*

He continued on toward Maraig…toward her. Twice, he stopped and thought about going back to England, or New York, or Tahiti. The Red had left. He wasn't coming back. River didn't need him to look after her. What if he lost his heart to her? How many years would they have? He didn't want that life. He wanted to fly. He'd always wanted to. Now that he could, what the hell was he doing here smelling grass and thinking of hunting Drakkon?

Still, he let his feet lead him onward toward the woman who made him forget flying.

CHAPTER SEVEN

"ARE YOU GOING to tell me what he's doing here?"

River turned her gaze away from the kitchen window and Mr. Wilder heading up the road, and gave her sister a solemn look. What was she going to tell Ivy? How long could she keep her secret from her sister? Ivy would have laughed and called her fanciful, but now with Mr. Wilder here to confirm the truth, how would poor Ivy react? Finding out dragons were real and very dangerous was life changing.

"He's here to find out what killed our cattle."

"And burned the land," Ivy reminded her.

"Yes."

"Da thinks it was the dragon. He's afraid."

River looked into her sister's wide, blue eyes painted in dark shades of makeup. The shadows couldn't hide Ivy's anxiety. Like River, she had grown up hearing their father's dragon tale. She'd grown afraid of it, too, though she'd never admit it. Ivy tried to appear unaffected by things, but River knew her twin better than anyone. Their mother leaving had affected them both tremendously. Ivy stayed with the same guy she'd grown up with and River stayed home. They shared everything and River felt guilty for not telling Ivy about the dragon. She wanted to protect her sister from the gravity of knowing the truth. But being oblivious to danger didn't make one safe.

He knocked at the front door. River hurried to answer it, thankful for the distraction. She swung it open and looked up to find Mr. Wilder turned toward the sky.

Hearing her, he turned his head, giving her a glorious display of his strong profile against the sun. His eyes settled on her and darkened to smoky sapphire. "Hello."

For a moment, River felt consumed by fire and cherished in the flames. When he slanted his smile at her and went altogether awkward again, she almost fanned herself. "Hi," she replied, smiling back.

"I was right," he said, his eyes cooling and flicking to Ivy, who appeared at the door. "Your cattle were killed by a gang from Lewis. We've had a problem with them stealing cattle in the past. They recently started burning farms and mutilating the cattle."

"Are the police coming?" Ivy asked.

"No," he told her, thinking fast on his feet. "We're not notifying the police since the crime scene has been tampered with. I don't want anyone to get into trouble."

"Thanks," Ivy offered. "Who do you work for?"

"The government," River told her. "All of them," she added when she thought Ivy might ask that next. "Mr. Wilder," she said, offering him a smile. "Please, come in." She stepped aside to allow him entry. "My sister, Ivy, was just about to fetch my father from the pub."

"It's early," he remarked softly, entering the house.

"It's been a difficult morning for him. We are now poor."

He shook his head. "My organization has purchased cattle from a farm in Glengorm, well known for their prime Scotch beef, to replace what you lost. They should arrive in the next couple of weeks."

"Seriously?" Ivy asked, her eyes, as well as her smile were wider than usual while her gaze cut to her sister. "That had to cost a fortune."

"It's nothing," he replied, making light of it. "It won't make a dent in their pockets."

"Thank you," River told him, unable to believe what he was saying. They weren't going under because of him? It was too much to owe a person. She should refuse, but her father…

"Ivy, go get Da. He's going to want to hear this."

She watched her sister head out the door and then beckoned Mr. Wilder to the sitting room. "Can I get you something to drink? Eat?"

"No," he said, taking off his pack and jacket and taking a seat on a small sofa. "We should talk before they get back."

River couldn't stop her gaze from taking in the broad flare of his shoulders in his tapered button-down shirt. "Of course," she said soberly and sat across from him on another larger sofa.

"There is another dragon. A Red. My people know of it now and have informed me that it's been spotted in the French Alps."

"So we're safe?"

He nodded. "I'd like to stay around for a few days just to make certain. I've taken a room at the B&B."

Why? Why was he doing all this for them? Why was he being so truthful about the dragons? She would have thought this would be more like a *Men In Black* thing. Was he going to pull out a wand and zap her memories clear?

His lips curled into a devastatingly charming smile that burned her insides and made her want to go to her room and compose something. Who was he? Who did he work for? Would he really kill Drakkon?

"You said you knew where the Red dragon was. What about the White?"

The front door burst open and Ivy reentered the house with Hagen Wray trailing behind his energetic daughter.

After brief introductions, River hurried off to make some tea, mostly for her father. Ivy followed her into the kitchen to inform her that she was going to the Munroe's farm to see Graham and tell him the good news.

"Mr. Wilder is seriously gorgeous, River," she whispered into River's ear before planting a kiss on her sister's cheek. "He seems nice and he has a freaking great job. Do something about it."

River only laughed and swatted her away. What was she supposed to do? Throw herself at him? No, she'd done that with Colin and he didn't respect her enough to call her when she left. She also couldn't forget the fact that, despite what he'd done for her family, he was a dragon hunter and he'd kill Drakkon if given the chance. She didn't want him to. Drakkon was magic come to life. He was beautiful and terrifying, and rare.

"What's this I hear about you replacing my cattle?" she heard her father ask when she returned to the sitting room with a tray.

"Not me, Mr. Wray," the hunter told him. His demeanor had changed to one of respect and politeness, but his voice was still husky and low and dangerous to her bones. "The people I work for."

"And the police aren't coming?" her father asked, taking his cup. "Smells like a cover-up to me and you're paying us off to keep quiet."

"Da!" River admonished gently. He was obviously drunk. She hoped the stranger didn't take too much offense.

Mr. Wilder looked a bit taken aback, but then he smiled. "It's all right."

"I've seen it happen before," her father insisted. "Twenty-two years ago. After the blue dragon flew into that man's window. I saw it all. I know what happened, but it all went away. The body, even the glass on the streets. It was all gone in an hour and nothing appeared in the papers."

"You saw a dragon?" Wilder asked her father, looking as stunned as if someone had told him that dragons were real.

"I sure as hell did. It was blue—or green with purple-tipped scales and it blocked out the sun. That's what made me look up. Other people saw it, too. I don't know why they never went public with it. They must have been paid off." Her father's bloodshot eyes roved over Mr. Wilder's near-white mane. "He had hair like yours, with less color maybe."

"The dragon?" Wilder asked, his gaze fixed on her father.

"No. The man who jumped, or was thrown out the penthouse window," her father replied, proving he wasn't so drunk after all. "He had white hair. I know what you want me to believe, but I'm not crazy."

"We know that, Da," River comforted him, moving closer to him on the sofa and putting her arm around him. She'd always believed that he believed what he'd seen. He wouldn't have risked losing his wife and the respect of his friends if he didn't. She'd never mocked him for it or asked him to stop telling people about it. But she had never considered the weight of what he carried, until now. She hadn't told him about seeing the White dragon. He would tell everyone they knew, anyone who listened—and she'd made a deal.

"I'm not here to make you believe anything, Mr. Wray," Wilder said gently. "You saw what you saw."

River wanted to smile at him for handling her father so delicately, but this was serious business and she didn't want to appear the grinning fool.

"Right," her father laughed. "And now you want us to believe a gang of kids did this. Do you know the power it takes to tear an eighteen hundred pound bull in half? You might not be here to change the truth, but you aren't here to bring it. So keep your cattle and leave my house."

"Da, you don't understand," River told him in a soothing voice. She couldn't let him do this. Wilder was protecting them by covering it up. "Please, let me explain."

"Miss Wray," Wilder interrupted, "please, let me."

She turned to him, hoping he would comfort her father with the truth—to verify that he wasn't insane.

He tugged at the stray hair falling down his cheek. "This is some kind of birth thing. My sister's hair was whiter than mine. It was handed down to us by our father, the...ehm..." he paused as if what he meant to say were too difficult. "...the man who jumped or was thrown from the window. He was my father. It's a long, complicated tale that I won't bore you with now."

His father? River thought, staring at him. What the hell...? It was too much of a coincidence. Unless it was all an elaborate lie and he was a wacko. Had she let a crazy guy into her home because he was drop-dead gorgeous and he knew weird stuff about dragons? No. He knew too much. He knew about Drakkon, and this new one, the Red. It would make sense that he'd be a dragon hunter since his father had been killed by one.

If he was who he said he was, then everything her father claimed he saw was true. He'd never denied it despite what it cost him.

"And the beast that killed him?" her father asked on a whispered breath.

River swiped her nose. She knew what hearing this meant to her father. Validation.

"Marrkiya, the Aqua."

Her father whimpered and River drew him in closer. He looked stunned and relieved, as if the weight of a twenty-two-year-old truth had been removed. "Marrkiya, the Aqua," he said, giving the monster that haunted him its name. "Seeing it was…" He rubbed his eyes and shook his head. "It was this impossible thing come to life. Terrifying and beautiful. I felt as if I'd stepped out of this world and into another."

"I've heard stories of Marrkiya's power and beauty," Mr. Wilder told him in his quiet voice. "What did you see the dragon do?"

River's father didn't hesitate to answer. He never had—but this time he had a willing, believing listener.

"I heard him first. His wings. I could hear them because everything else got quiet."

River nodded. Everything had gone silent just before she had seen Drakkon move.

"His great size cast a shadow on the streets, the windows, the people looking up. About seven of us saw him flying, his deadly talons opening as he broke through the window. Glass fell everywhere. Folks started screaming. More people looked up. I know they saw it, but no one would come forward after a few days. I did though. And it changed my whole life."

"How did it change your life?" Mr. Wilder asked him in his softly spoken voice.

"No one believed me. My friends laughed at me and finally drifted away. My wife could not stomach the ridicule and left me and the girls."

"I'm sorry," the hunter said.

"And we're sorry about your father," River told him. "What had he done to Marrkiya to make the dragon go through a window for him? Was your father simply in the wrong place at the wrong time, or was there more to it than that?"

"There was more to it than that. But as I said, it's a long, complicated story."

She watched how his tongue peeked out of the corner of his
mouth when he finished speaking—shy yet sensual. Like him. How
could a man who looked like he did be shy? She realized it was part of
his charm—what made him so believable.

"I'd like to hear it sometime," she said, her curiosity genuinely
piqued. Dragons were shrouded in mystery and legend as ancient as
time itself. She'd love to know more about them. Would Mr. Wilder
tell her? Would Drakkon? She was grateful to Wilder for telling her
father the truth, but why was he telling them so much?

He curled one end of his mouth at her. "Maybe later?"

Maybe.

"Where is the Aqua now?" her father asked him, breaking River's
thoughts of spending more time with Mr. Wilder.

"He is no more. You have nothing to fear."

"I'm not afraid. I'm just happy you believe me." Her father smiled
genuinely for the first time since his wife left him.

"I do," the hunter said.

Her father's smile faded "Your father…"

Mr. Wilder held up his hand to stop him. "I didn't know him. But
because of his death, an organization of hunters was formed, trained in
the art of taking down dragons. That's why I'm here. But it's safest if
we keep this and everything I told you quiet. People know about
them. Let that satisfy you."

"It does," her father promised with tear-filled eyes. "It finally
does." He quickly gathered himself and set down his cup and straightened his shoulders. "It was a dragon that killed my livestock, then.
How many of them are there, and how afraid should we be?"

"There are very few," Mr. Wilder told him, "and our tracking
devices show that the one that did this is gone. As I told your daughter, I've taken a room in Tarbert and will stay for a few days just to
make certain all is well. And you're correct. I am covering up the fact

that it was a dragon or you'll have people here you won't like."

"Yes, yes, you're right," her father agreed. "And about the cattle, tell your people I'll accept them."

Mr. Wilder caught her eye and shared a slight smile with her.

"But it's you I want to thank, young man." Hagan Wray rose to his feet. "Thank you for the truth." He held out his hand as Wilder stood with him. "I'm in your debt."

"No," the handsome hunter smiled and shook his head. "You are not."

River wanted to thank him, too. She didn't want to like him, but she did. She understood why he was a hunter. A dragon had killed his father. She wanted to know why. It chilled her blood but part of her suspected there was a reason the Aqua had singled out Mr. Wilder's father. How much did Jacob know about dragons? How could one man stand up against such a mighty force? She wanted to ask him, to find out everything.

"I think I'm going to lie down for a bit," her father announced. "It's been an eventful day and the sun hasn't even gone down yet. I have much to think about. You'll stay for dinner."

"Thank you."

The hunter was staying for dinner. What would Drakkon think?

River rose from the sofa and kissed her father on the cheek then watched him wander off to his room. He walked with a bit more of a bounce in his step. She didn't know if he was happier about his livelihood being given back to him, or because he was finally able to talk about his dragon with someone who truly believed him.

Alone again with the kind stranger, she smiled a little breathlessly when she caught him staring at her. "I appreciate what you did for him…and for Ivy. It's almost hard to believe you're a trained killer."

"I haven't killed any yet," he replied, spreading his curious gaze over her features. "You sound like you don't approve."

It was the way he looked at her, as if her answer mattered to him for some reason. Why should it? Why would he care if she approved of him or not? "It's not that," she admitted, weighing her words carefully while she tucked her hair behind her ear. "But if a dragon is peaceful and almost extinct, why not let it live?"

"The reasons are piled in your friend, Noah's truck."

"But the White didn't do it."

His gaze softened on her. She suddenly felt like the room was too small. Did he move a little closer? His scent washed over her, like the morning dew with a hint of spice. "You protect him." His voice rolled across her ears like the waves of a fathomless sea.

She crossed her arms over her chest, but it provided no defense against his slow, beautiful smile. "I would protect anything that was innocent."

"You saw Drakkon." Now, he did take a step forward, closer. "What was he like?"

She stared up into his cloudless, blue eyes, the silky thread of palest gold falling around his hard, angular jaw. "Like you," she said softly, then blinked and laughed at herself. She sounded as crazy as people accused her father of being. "I mean he was big and white and his eyes—"

Ivy entered the house in a whirlwind of blue hair and cigarette smoke. River scowled at her when Ivy hurried toward her. "Were you smoking?"

"No, Graham was, but listen, Graham's band needs new music—"

"No," River told her. She'd heard Graham's band and nothing she wrote suited the head banger's style.

"If they want to use something you wrote," her sister continued, "they'll pay five hundred to buy it."

Five hundred was a good chunk to put towards her future. But her work as heavy metal? "I don't think it's a right fit, Ivy."

"Please, River," her sister begged. "Just let him play something and then decide." She turned to Mr. Wilder. "What do you think?"

He nodded, keeping his eyes on River. "Let him play something."

River thought about it. She hated saying no to Ivy, and Ivy knew it. She knew how to play those big, blue eyes to her best advantage.

"You never know," her sister went on. "Your song could be a great hit for Graham's band. It could launch his career, and yours."

River doubted it, but...she did have something new. It had taken her almost two months to compose and it still wasn't finished. It was something wild and as untamable as the wind. Something inspired by a force of nature. "I may have something that will fit Graham's style. It's almost done."

Ivy squealed and threw her arms around her. "I'll go tell Graham that we'll see him at the barn with the music tonight."

River nodded and caught Mr. Wilder smiling as her sister rushed back out. She eyed his clothes, his expensive boots. He probably had never heard music outside of a grand theatre. "I'm told the barn has good acoustics."

"Barns are great for band practice. I miss playing in one."

"Oh?" she asked, eyebrows lifted. "You play?"

"I was the lead guitarist with *Everbound.*"

Her eyes opened wider. A dragon hunter/musician. What other surprises did he plan on springing on her? "I've heard of them! You guys are pretty popular. Why did you leave?"

He shrugged. "Just time for something new."

Something new. The music in her room. Oh, she'd love a professional opinion. Drakkon loved her work but this one was different. "Would you like to hear my song?"

He inhaled, looking uncertain. "I shouldn't. I have...ehm...things to—"

"Please," she said softly and added a smile when he finally nodded.

CHAPTER EIGHT

J ACOB'S LEGS FELT weighted to the ground and, with every step he
forced his feet to take back to the sofa, his head shouted for him to
go the other way. He should leave now while he was still a man. He
remembered the last time he'd heard River's music. What if he
transformed right here in her sitting room? She thought he looked like
Drakkon. Could he ever tell her that he *was* Drakkon? He should go,
before things got more complicated. But he stayed, watching River
disappear down the hall.

What was he doing getting deeper and deeper into her life? Replacing her cattle, telling her and her father about Garion's foster father,
Marrkiya, sitting here waiting for her to sing to him. His head wanted
him to run, to fly. But his heart refused to let him.

He'd lied to her about Red being in the French Alps. He didn't
want to scare her. He'd stay for a few days and make sure Red wasn't
coming back. And then he'd leave.

But presently, he sat back down.

He thought about her father seeing Marrkiya. Helena had told him
in Fiji that Marrkiya, the last of the ancients that Jacob's father had
transformed, had been the one responsible for Patrick White's death.
And he knew why. He didn't blame Marrkiya. He didn't know why
he'd agreed to tell River.

He'd probed Hagan Wray just a bit, enough to understand the
effect seeing Marrkiya had had on his life. He knew nothing he said
was going to change the man's mind, so he hadn't tried. Besides, he'd
sensed River's heartache for her father. He'd wanted to help.

Why hadn't she told him about her father seeing the Aqua? That
made three Drakkon in this family's life. What were the chances of

that? Were the stars somehow involved? It would be a cruel twist of fate to meet the woman he was meant to be with, now that he was immortal. Now that he'd let her believe he and Drakkon were separate.

She returned a moment later holding her sheet music in one hand and an old guitar in the other. He watched her approach, unable to look anywhere else. He liked the way her glossy hair danced around her shoulders, the kindness and courage illuminating her eyes, her long, coltish legs.

"I thought you might play it on my guitar," she said, sitting next to him and handing him the sheet music. She continued speaking about tones and pitches, bars and bridges. He hardly heard any of it. It was too easy to lose himself in her large, soulful eyes. Her scent drew him closer. He wanted to take her in, drench himself in her fragrance. His eyes fastened on her lips while she spoke. Kissing her would be too dangerous. He was here to help. There could never be more than that. But he wanted to kiss her, taste her. Hell, he'd never wanted anything so bad. But what if the stars sang?

Helena had told him she'd heard the heavens sing when she'd first kissed Garion. It meant they were life mates, bound together for eternity. Good for them. They were both Drakkon. He didn't want to spend eternity with one woman. He didn't want to miss her for that long. Every day, each time he spoke to River, he grew more afraid. What if he lost his heart to her? He was afraid it might happen if they shared their breath in a kiss. He had to keep his control intact. His will could not fail him now. He was leaving soon.

"So if I use this chord—" She looked up from her music and into his eyes. "It should…" She paused, her naturally coral lips parted on a silent breath, then dipped her gaze, veiling her eyes behind long, black lashes.

What was he doing? He was scaring her. This wasn't him. He didn't behave like an awkward virgin around women. He was cool, detached, mysterious. This had to be Drakkon. "I'm sorry if I…" he said roughly and moved away.

She lifted her gaze back to him. He was tempted to probe her thoughts more deeply, but he'd promised her he wouldn't. "Who are you, Mr. Wilder? You hunt dragons and play lead guitar in your spare time—"

"It's the other way around," he corrected with a smile. She didn't approve of his hunting Drakkon. It was an odd surprise to hear from a human. A good surprise. "In fact, I spent many years avoiding hunting them."

"Then what changed?" she asked.

"I stumbled upon the White while I was vacationing in Fiji. I've been tracking him since."

"You hate him," she said with a heavy voice.

"No, I don't. I feel sorry for him actually. Imagine your entire race being eradicated and the only way you've survived is by staying hidden from the eyes that would want you dead if they saw you. The eyes of the entire world."

Not the entire world.

He heard her silent thought and tried not to smile. Not her. He turned his body to face her and lost the battle to remain stoic. "I sense a fair heart in you, Miss Wray."

A hint of scarlet brushed across her cheeks. It was real and rare. Would she still blush after years of being together?

"Call me River."

River.

He blinked and his eyes opened wider on her when he realized what he'd done. She blinked as well, hearing his voice in her head. He had to fix it.

What is this you're doing to the worm?

Drakkon?

Jacob watched, captivated by the faraway look in her eyes, the slightest shift in her breath when she spoke to Drakkon.

"River," he said softly, pulling her from other thoughts.

Her gaze focused on him and she smiled.

"But sympathizing with them," he continued, "doesn't change the truth. We can't let them refill the sky. Mankind wouldn't survive it."

She nodded but looked away. *Is he right, Drakkon? Would dragons turn on mankind?*

Eventually, yes. The strongest survive.

You would let them kill me?

He should tell her that he was Drakkon. He didn't care what other Drakkon did. But it wasn't true. That's why he was here. He cared. About her.

No, I wouldn't.

She relaxed her shoulders and Jacob was tempted to touch them, to help her with the weight she carried.

"Do you think the Red will try to contact the White? To join forces or something?"

"No," he told her. "The Reds are warriors. They share different beliefs than the Whites, whose purpose in the days of the ancients was to keep the peace." He stopped for a moment, then exhaled, then raked his fingers through his hair. "It's a complicated tale."

"Yes," she smiled at him. "And you still haven't told me the first complicated tale about your father."

"He stole Marrkiya's treasure."

Her eyes opened wide, compelling him to look deeper into them. "Why? Why would he do that?"

"Because he was a fool."

"What was the treasure?" she asked breathlessly, caught up in the story.

"I'm told it was a woman."

Her lips parted and his gaze dipped there. "The dragon loved a woman?"

"It's mostly rumor," he told her. "I won't go on."

"I don't mind."

Neither did he. That was the problem. He could sit here on her sofa with her and tell her everything. He was telling her too much. Why? Why was he continuing this game of Drakkon and the lady? He was leaving, wasn't he?

"Let's see what we have here," he said veering away from the topic. He reached out and took the guitar from her hands, grazing his fingertips over hers way back, hovering close. He probed. Her thoughts were of him.

When he set the guitar in his lap and played a few strings, he cringed.

"It's old."

"It's just out of tune," he assured her with a tender glance. "I can fix it." She'd been content to compose on this thing. He could try to make it sing. He wondered how she could compose music and not be able to tune a guitar. Unless, "You don't play?"

She shook her head. "It hurts my fingers, but Ivy plays a little. I prefer a piano."

He dragged his gaze off her and looked around. He didn't see a piano anywhere. She should have one.

"Do you play anything besides the guitar?" she asked, pulling his attention back to her. How could she think she was plain? Hell, she was mesmerizing, sapping him of strength to resist her.

He nodded. "A few things. My sister is the true musician though. She plays violin for the New York Philharmonic."

The little gasp that parted her lips made him forget what he was doing.

"That's amazing," she said. "Your family must be very proud of both of you."

"We have no family," he said and finished tuning the guitar. He set the sheet music between him and River on the sofa and, without any further explanation about his past, began to play. The melody started off soft but then grew heavy, chaotic, a driving force that drew him in and clung to him like vines, tethering him to her.

Her music spoke of something dark and out of control, of longing for the elusive. How did she know? How did she write music that captured who he was?

The only thing that kept him from altering was concentrating on the notes, the chords—and, thankfully, his training in Skye. She hadn't written an ending, so he added one of his own.

Done, he put the guitar down and kept his gaze hidden beneath his long lashes. Drakkon was close. Jacob could feel the fire burning his eyes. It wanted her. Its feral desire clenched his muscles and stiffened his bones. What would Drakkon do to her besides scare her to death? He had to control it. If he was ever going to tell her the truth about who he was, this wasn't the time.

"Are you all right?" she asked, leaning in to place her hand on his arm.

He nodded and looked at her as the embers died down in his eyes.

"Did you like it?" she asked a little breathless. "I did," she admitted with a soft laugh. "You made it sound better than when it was in my head."

"You just need a better guitar."

"No, you were feeling it," she told him, though he was sure she hadn't probed his thoughts. "I could see it on your face. You played it with the passion it needed and it sounded really good. I love the ending. Graham is going to like it."

"He's crazy if he doesn't but why would you sell it for so little?"

She shrugged her delicate shoulders. "Because it's what the band can afford, and I have plenty more songs."

"Good, because I could probably help you license them and get them into the right hands."

Her eyes widened on him, along with her smile, addling his thoughts for a minute. "Why?"

"Because you're talented."

"Millions of people are talented," she countered quietly. "You've already done too much."

One corner of his mouth hooked up in a curious smile. "Too much for what?"

"To ever repay you."

"Who said anything about repaying me?"

She tilted her head to get a better look at him, then finally turned on the sofa to face him. "Are you an angel? I mean, if dragons are real…"

He breathed out a husky laugh. "Far from it."

"Then what's behind your protection and help?"

She certainly had a suspicious nature, didn't she? Jacob didn't know what to answer, so he went with the truth. It hardly ever worked in the past, but River was different.

"I like you," he said, leaning in slightly. The urge to kiss her, to smell her overwhelmed him. She wanted it too, leaning in with him. Her mouth was close. He could smell tea on her breath and vanilla in her hair. He moved in closer, tempted to run his fingertips over the alluring curve of her jaw, to brush his lips over hers, to spread his tongue over the seam of her mouth.

No. He didn't want to hear the stars, and he believed he would if he kissed her.

He withdrew hesitantly. Denying himself the pleasures of a woman wasn't something he was familiar with, but he fought his will and won.

"I should go," he said, moving off the sofa.

"To Tarbert?" she asked. The disappointment in her voice drew him back. "How can you protect me from Tarbert?"

She was either truly afraid of dragons, which was a good thing, or she didn't want him to leave for other reasons. From what he knew of her so far, she didn't frighten easily. Hell, he couldn't help but crook his mouth up at her pretty face. She made him stop thinking of anything else but her. What about flying? His dream had finally come true and here he was, grounded to the earth by a woman of all things! She made him feel weak and willing to do anything, even lie to her, just to be near her. "I was going to go outside and look around."

"Oh." Her soft voice fell across his ears. "Well, I guess I'll see you later then."

"Unless," he said, despite every warning going off in his head, "you'd care to join me."

CHAPTER NINE

J ACOB WILDER WAS a peculiar man with an odd affinity for small, round stones. He'd plucked a number of them from the bank of Loch Seaforth beyond the village where they walked, examined them and, finding them unworthy, tossed them back down. Who was he? Where did he come from? How had he known about the attack so quickly? River had never heard of generous government agents or rock star dragon hunters. Would he really try to help her with her music? It was her deepest desire. He seemed to know her, to know exactly what she needed. He was open with her, telling her much more than she ever would have dreamed. He liked her. He told her so and, heaven help her, she'd nearly melted all over her sofa.

She liked him, too, despite one of his occupations.

But he was guarded as well, introverted, with introspective depth, protecting his secrets behind the armor of his radiant smile, the deep timbre of his voice, the sexy rumble of his laughter. He hunted Drakkon because he thought it was the right thing to do, and maybe it was. But he didn't hate them and he played music she'd composed for one with passion that brought her music to life. He'd stopped himself from kissing her—and he'd wanted to. She had seen it in his eyes, consuming her in blue-gold flames. She could feel his desire for her coming off him in waves, but there was something else. Something that stopped him. Apprehension. Fear. Of what?

It was all so…peculiar.

"What are you looking for?" she asked him while they walked. Did dragons leave evidence behind? Like a tooth, or a scale? Should she go look around the crag where she'd first seen Drakkon? "Why aren't there any footprints?"

"It never landed," he answered, bending to pick something up from the ground.

River's heart pounded at the thought of a dragon hovering over her farm sometime during the night. It could have easily swung its head around and burned her house down with her family inside. It wasn't her peaceful White but a warrior Red that had attacked. She'd thought Drakkon was guilty. For some mad reason, she wasn't afraid of Drakkon. She hadn't considered the full threat of what had happened. That it was a different, more aggressive beast that had swooped down upon her little farm, not even bothering to land to kill everything. That there were more of them. She hadn't wanted to consider it. The Red dragon had cooked and eaten her cattle. It could have easily eaten her and her father, and Ivy. She stopped walking and clutched her belly as everything hit her at once.

Jacob looked up from a round stone he was inspecting and abandoned his task to go to her.

"Are you sure the Red dragon is in the French Alps?" she asked him when he reached her.

"Yes," he said covering her hand with his, still at her belly.

His touch soothed her and sent sparks through her nerves at the same time. She looked up at him and noted how the gold streaks in his hair glimmered under the sun. He was radiant…like a star, or an angel.

"Don't worry," he spoke on a sorcerer's whisper, his eyes seeing through her to her fear. "I won't let it hurt you or your family."

She wanted to believe him. But he was just a man. It should be Drakkon offering his help. "How can you stop it?"

He smiled and lifted his fingers to a lock of her hair to clear it from her eyes. "Trust me, River."

Trust him? She didn't even know him. She looked into his eyes. What was it she saw there, heard in his deep, breathy voice? "You…" She paused, knowing she would sound insane. "You say my name like…"

Should she admit to him that she communicated with Drakkon? Would he laugh at her? Would he drill her and try to use her to trap the dragon? "This is all a lot to take in."

"I know," he said, his resonant voice imbued with compassion. He lowered his hand from her. He didn't need it to still her breath. He used his gaze to touch her, to search her. "Tell me about your music. What inspires you?"

She knew what he was doing and she welcomed it. She didn't want to think about dragons—bad ones or good ones. She needed a break from all the insanity for a few hours. She wanted to enjoy the company of a beautiful man whose smile was like the sun rising after a hard night. A man who wanted to help her get her music out there, who'd gotten his organization to replace her father's cattle, and who'd committed himself to protecting her and her family. A man who wanted to know about her music.

"This inspires me. All of it." She waved her free hand around her and smiled remembering that she was a bit peculiar, too. "There's music in the roll of the waves and in the howling hum of the wind. Nature is a perfect balance of power and delicacy." She felt her cheeks flush when she caught him smiling, watching her, listening.

"Go on," he urged softly.

It felt good to toss off the burdens of her everyday, ordinary life and talk to someone about her music instead of what was for dinner or what else they could bring into the shop to attract more customers. Meeting Drakkon had brought something magical and exciting into her life, but she could never tell anyone about him. He lived in her memory, and it wasn't enough.

Jacob Wilder was real and he was here.

"Only one man has ever heard it—besides you now." And a dragon.

His smile faltered. "What man? Did you love him?"

"Just a guy I knew from University. And I thought I did." Why was she even talking about Colin? She thought of him from time to time because there wasn't much else to think about. "He turned out to be a jerk."

"And a fool."

"Yes," she agreed with a soft smile. "He was. But I'm glad that things worked out the way they did. He wasn't right for me."

"How do you know?"

She cut him a playful glance and picked up her steps. "Because I'm much too complex for Colin's simple brain. He didn't like my music."

He looked so offended on her behalf she almost giggled. "Really?" he growled. "I'll make certain he knows when you're famous."

"Do you really think it's good?" she asked. "Ivy and Colin are the only opinions I've heard until now. I mean, I'm confident it's good. It comes from my heart, but you know this type of thing."

"I do, and that's why I'm telling you, Colin is a deaf fool."

She laughed. It felt easy with him. Like when she and Noah laughed together, which they hardly ever did anymore. But she'd never wanted to kiss Noah. She'd never wanted to stare into Noah's eyes for the rest of her life, or think of ways to make him smile. But she knew nothing about Jacob Wilder.

"Tell me about you," she said. "You said you had no family. Where did you grow up?"

He continued walking for a bit, looking unsure about what to tell her. Why would he find it easier to talk about secret organizations and dragons than about his personal life?

"I didn't mean to pry—"

"No, it's all right," he said, sounding like the wind. "I've never told this to anyone. I never thought I would. I'm unprepared."

He'd never told anyone? Why was he telling her? He could have refused and remained mysterious, though she doubted his life story would reveal all about him.

"My parents died when I was three. Helena was two. We were the youngest of my father's brood." He paused in his words and his steps for a moment and cut his gaze to her. He lifted his brow as if expecting her to question him further. When she didn't, he let his eyes dip to the ground and continued walking. "He was a wealthy man and had provided for us, should we be orphaned, which we were. We were shipped off to different countries for five years, raised by different nurses and teachers and then brought to live with our half-brother, Hendrick. At the time, Hendrick was the head of our organization, The Bane, dedicated to hunting dragons. We lived with him for three years until a dragon burned down our house and almost half my relatives with it. After that, we were mostly on our own."

She stepped back. A dragon? A dragon had killed his father *and* his home and his family. She had a sinking feeling that there was much more to all this than he was telling her. She would have thought he'd hate dragons with a burning passion. She knew she would have felt that way had it been her father and family. "I'm so sorry," she said quietly. "I'm sorry I brought it up."

He quirked his mouth. "Why?"

"It causes you pain."

"No, it doesn't."

"Jacob. You lost your whole family to a dragon. How could it not cause you pain?"

"I hardly knew them. Helena is my family, and we both escaped."

She swallowed. He spoke like nothing fazed him. She wasn't buying it. "You enjoy being mysterious."

His low laughter filled her ears and made her eyes burn.

He stepped closer and watched as a breeze blew tendrils of her hair over her lips, beckoning his gaze, his fingers there. She didn't back away when he spread his fingertips over her bottom lip and a hundred different visions of him kissing her flitted across her thoughts. He appeared as entranced as she, as if he saw the same visions and was about to make them all come true. He dipped his chin slightly, lifting his eyes to hers at the same time. Fire shone in their depths, wild and uncontainable. The heat consumed her, seeping into the farthest chasms of her heart. She had the urge to tip her head back and offer him her throat.

His nostrils flared slightly and he leaned in a little closer, enough that she felt his warm breath against her jaw.

"Ask me whatever you want."

How could her heart pound so madly for a man she'd met this

morning? What was this power he wielded so expertly over her that tempted her to tell him to *take* whatever he wanted.

"Is your heart spoken for?" She scowled, wondering when she'd lost control over her mouth.

But just when she began to defend her foolish tongue, he severed his gaze from hers and withdrew. "No, it's not."

She watched him take a step back, looking uncomfortable and uncertain. He furrowed his brow and then looked at her from beneath its shadow.

River wanted to say something but suddenly her rogue tongue went silent. What was wrong with him? What was this nerve she touched? Had someone he loved dumped him? Was he still in love? In denial? She understood the painful process off getting over someone. It wasn't—

His expression softened and his eyes went starkly blue and a little apprehensive. "Is yours?"

She shook her head. "No."

He quirked his mouth into something that could have been a smile of relief, or a contortion of terror. Either way, he swung around and continued walking.

Like she said...peculiar. But he made her smile and she wasn't even sure why.

She picked up her steps and caught up with him. "Tell me more about your life," she said, looking up and taking in the strength of his profile.

He glanced at her and his smile widened. "You would know everything then?"

Yes. Yes, she wanted to know everything about him. What were his favorite things? Why did talking about his heart make him go dark, but talking about the death of his family members had barely stirred him. "You said I could ask," she reminded him, her smile matching his.

"It's not good, I'm afraid. I got into trouble a lot. I drove Helena nuts. I finally landed a job modeling and then I met the guys from the band. That's it. Nothing exciting."

"Nothing exciting? You travel with the band, don't you? You've been places, met people—"

"Is that what you want to do? Travel and meet people?"

"Yes, it's my dream to spread my wings and—" She laughed at herself. "That's probably not the best metaphor. I just know there's more than this."

"There is," he agreed. "Why don't you leave? Your family?"

She shook her head and stayed quiet for a minute, not sure she wanted to share this part of her life with him. "It's partially the money," she told him, wondering why it was so easy to share this...and her music with him.

"And the other part?" he asked in his slow, deep voice that was beginning to sound like music to her ears.

"To be honest, I don't know if I can make it out there on my own. It's scary."

"You don't strike me as someone who lets fear or uncertainty get in her way."

She laughed and bumped his arm. He didn't budge. "You don't know anything about me."

He leaned in and said above her ear, "Then tell me."

Should she? He wasn't staying in Harris. She didn't want to start caring for a guy only to be dumped again. And she was pretty sure that if she fell for Jacob Wilder, she'd fall hard. Besides his tender attentiveness, he was beyond gorgeous, and he played music. He was shy and confident at the same time, which beguiled the senses right out of her. He was thoughtful and generous—yet there was something terribly dangerous about him that she couldn't put her finger on, something familiar and feral in his burning eyes and the glint of hunger in them when he looked at her.

Don't eat me!

No. What she was thinking couldn't be true. Dragon shape-shifters weren't real. They were the products of twenty-first century romance authors' imaginations. Then again, dragons weren't supposed to be real either. They were products of centuries old authors. Same thing.

She looked at Jacob walking beside her, farther away than he'd been a moment before. He lifted his eyes from the ground and then dragged his hand over his head, clearing his hair from his vision to look at her.

"I think…I think things are moving too fast." Hell, that was the hardest thing she'd had to say in two years. Was she crazy? Dragon shape-shifters? Seriously?

"Okay." He turned away—a bit ruffled. Was it her rejection that unsettled him…or something else?

"I'm sorry, it's just—"

"You're right." He stopped her and returned his gaze to hers. "Things are moving too fast. I'm glad," he said, aiming the crook of his disarming smile straight at her, "that at least one of us is clear-headed."

She stared at his mouth while he spoke. She wanted to laugh at his claim. She'd believed for a moment that he was Drakkon, and for half that time, she didn't care. She was anything but clear-headed.

CHAPTER TEN

J ACOB STOOD ON the top of the hill overlooking the loch and thought about the woman cooking dinner inside the house behind him. She suspected he was Drakkon. How? What had he done to raise her suspicions? His hair? The way he said her name? Was that enough to question his humanity? He should tell her the truth. Part of him wanted to. He'd already told her much. More than he probably should. About dragons. About himself.

What more would he have told her had she asked? He'd offered to answer anything. But she'd asked about his heart being spoken for and it had affected him in a way that was totally foreign to him. Fear had engulfed him. Fear that perhaps his heart was spoken for and she was the one claiming it.

Why now? Why her?

No one knew him. He'd never let anyone get close enough to know him. He'd never spoken about his childhood, about never belonging anywhere or to anyone. He never wanted to speak of it again. But he'd wanted to tell her. He wanted her to know at least some part of him, since he knew so much about her. He knew her dreams—the ones in her heart, and the ones in her head. Music...and Colin with the black hair.

The parts of her mind that he'd touched proved she didn't love Colin.

But she still dreamed of him.

What would he do about it? Nothing. He'd do nothing. She didn't belong to him. This wasn't the seventeenth century. She wasn't a possession. This was Drakkon thinking and it was dangerous.

He heard a sound behind him and took a deep breath in. The faint scent of cigarette smoke drifted across his nostrils. Ivy. He turned to see her walking up the hill toward him. She was shorter than River by at least seven or eight inches. Her eyes, beneath the hood of her sweatshirt were large and tainted with cynicism. Jacob wondered how she had grown so distrustful. Then he remembered Hagan Wray's words His wife had left them. People he'd called friends had mocked him. Because of a dragon.

"I like it here," she said, coming to stand beside him and gazing at the water. "Sometimes I feel like there's a fire inside my soul and I want to jump into the sea and let it douse the flames."

He glanced at her, wondering what emotions roiled within her.

She turned to look at him. "What are you still doing here, Mr. Wilder?"

"Call me Jacob."

"Sure. What are you still doing here, Jacob?" she asked, her eyes round and suspicious. "Are you expecting the gang to come back?"

He smiled. "They might."

She cast him a doubtful look and came to stand beside him, her gaze spread out over the loch. "Why is your hair white?"

"Why is yours blue?"

She smiled, still not looking at him. "River tells me you were the lead guitarist for *Everbound*, but you left because…?"

"It was time."

She cut him another skeptical glance. "Speaking of time, how did you manage time to work for all the governments and a top-charting band?"

She was clever. He liked her. "It was difficult."

She sighed and folded her arms across her chest and was silent for a moment. Then, "Do you like River?"

"Yes."

Now, she turned to him, her expression of surprise making his smile deepen. "I wasn't expecting you to be so truthful, Jacob."

"I know," he said quietly. "I wasn't expecting it either." He quirked his mouth at himself and then set his eyes toward the sun. He should be flying across it, heading someplace warmer, less inhabited. But instead, he was standing here at the edge of a tiny village waiting to eat dinner with a woman and her family. "It's obvious really."

"She likes you, too."

He slid his gaze back to her. "How do you know?" Why did he care? Wasn't it worse if she liked him, too? Wasn't he sentencing them both to heartache?

"She's cooking for you."

"She cooked for Noah," he countered.

Ivy searched his gaze and then smiled, discovering more about him than he wanted to let on. "But she's cooking her best dishes tonight."

"Is she?" he breathed. No one had ever cooked for him before. It was nice of her. But puzzling. She didn't want anything to happen between them. She said things were moving too fast. She was right. "I didn't mean to put her to more trouble."

"Oh," Ivy didn't bother to hold back her laughter. "I'm sure you're quite used to causing trouble wherever you go, Jacob." Her mirth faded and she set her somber gaze on his. "Just don't hurt my sister. Please."

The only way to agree was to leave Maraig right now. If he stayed and grew closer to her...if he kissed her and heard music...he should have been gone by now.

"Did someone hurt her?"

"Yes."

"Colin?"

Ivy nodded. "He was an asshole."

Drakkon? Are you there?

He heard River's sweet voice in his head and blinked at her sister. "You should get back. I'll be along in a few minutes."

"Sure," Ivy shrugged her petite shoulders and tugged her hood farther over her eyes. She turned away, but he called her back.

"Smoking will hurt you."

She looked like she was about to deny her habit, then rethought it, maybe because he'd been honest with her. She nodded then disappeared down the hill.

Where are you?

He closed his eyes while River beckoned him—as she'd beckoned since the first time they'd met.

I hope you're not asleep or...worse.

Worse? He felt his guts go warm at the sound of her concern in his head. He wanted to answer her, but it was better if he didn't. She was starting to find similarities between him and Drakkon. The more he spoke to her like this, the harder it would be to tell her the truth.

I just wanted you to know that Jacob...Mr. Wilder isn't so bad. I think I can convince him to leave you alone.

He smiled at her wanting to help him. What had Drakkon done to earn her loyalty?

Drakkon? What's wrong? Why won't you answer?

It took everything in him not to. It took even more to control Drakkon and not fly to her. If he'd wanted to strengthen his will, this was the way to do it. He turned around and walked back to the house.

THE AROMAS WAFTING through the house smelled so good it made Jacob feel lightheaded. He was starving. When he entered the kitchen, his eyes settled on River first, alone in the kitchen, cooking with her back to him. His gaze traversed the thick, ginger braid dangling down her long, elegant back. His eyes roved hungrily over her small derrière and then fell to the wooden dinner table arrayed with spring flowers, folded napkins, fine silverware, and glasses filled with white wine. Had she done all this for him? If she wanted to move more slowly, this wasn't the way to do it.

She turned from a steaming pot on the stove and smiled when she saw him. "Oh, good! You're here."

He decided then and there that it was his favorite thing she'd said to him.

"I was just about to call everyone in."

"Let me help you." He went to her. Drawn by her scent and the fragrance of the food behind her, he couldn't help himself.

"No, you're—" she stopped when he came close and reached behind her for the basket of baked rolls waiting to be set on the table. "—a guest." She spoke on a broken whisper against his jaw as he leaned in. He smiled and dipped his gaze to her lips. He wanted to close his arm around her and haul her in close. He wanted to feel her heart thrashing against his chest while he captured her, tasted her, branded her. He stepped back with the basket in his hand. He may be keeping Drakkon caged but he was thinking like something wild and more primitive. He'd felt it earlier at the loch, when he'd touched her mouth and filled her head with every way he wanted to kiss her. He'd felt himself losing to Drakkon when she thought about surrendering herself to him. She managed to find an opening in his armor. He didn't know how or what he should do about it. Was it already too late?

Soon, the others entered the kitchen and Jacob was seated to the left of the head of the table, opposite River and beside Ivy, who sat across from Graham, Noah's brother.

Much to Jacob's delight, River's dinner came in three courses. First, she served them mussels cooked in lemon and star anise sauce. It was better than anything he'd had in the finest restaurants. Conversation around the table flowed smoothly, with most of the questions aimed at him. How long had he been with *Everbound*? What other instruments did he play? What were some of the places he'd been? Why wasn't he drinking his wine?

"I have a bad reaction to alcohol," he explained. Bad, as in it could make him bed-ridden for a week or two. He looked across the table at River. He thought alcohol was the hardest thing he'd had to give up. He was wrong.

"Poor dude," Graham, who sported a neon green Mohawk, a few facial piercings, and a set of thoughtful eyes, said and sipped his wine.

They laughed over oven-roasted salmon with potato cakes, asparagus and lemon cream sauce, and stories, told by Mr. Wray, of his daughters' childish escapades and River's determination to attend

University.

After dinner, they retired to the sitting room with pear tarts and tea. This kind of quiet, settled life was completely foreign to Jacob. He hadn't eaten a home-cooked meal since he was eleven. There hadn't been any softly lit sitting rooms where family gathered in his past. He wasn't sure how he felt about it. It wasn't unpleasant, just unfamiliar. River was here, and that made everything else okay for some damned strange reason. She pulled him closer toward something. He wasn't sure what it was or what would happen when he got there.

Part of him didn't want to go. Didn't want to risk losing his heart to temporary love. He thought he could resist. Not caring had become second nature. But now that he was Drakkon, when he needed that wall to stay high and strong, he felt it shaking.

Another part of him, a part as foreign as family dinners and innocence, wanted her to take back what she said about moving too quickly. Wanted to kiss her senseless and to hell with the stars.

"Did you enjoy dinner?" she asked him, returning to the sofa after bidding her father goodnight and Ivy and Graham went back to the kitchen to clean up.

He let his eyes rove over her smile, her curious gaze. His gums itched and his chest burned. "I loved it. You compose beautiful music and cook like a master chef. What can't you do?"

"Stop," she said gently, patting his forearm that was resting on his thigh. "You don't need to flatter me."

"But I want to," he told her, surprised and beguiled by her humility. "I'm complimenting you."

Her easy smile returned, along with a rosy streak across her otherwise alabaster cheeks. "Well, thank you, but I can't play the guitar, and you've only heard one of my songs. The others are different."

He'd heard another song she'd hummed to him and he feared that it might have changed the course of his path. He was here with her instead of in Skye or on one of Fiji's remote islands flying.

He dipped his eyes to her hand still atop his forearm. She moved it away.

"Sorry, I—"

He tilted his head and tipped his smile at her. "You can touch me."

She stared at him for a moment, drawing a shallow breath. Then she looked away. What was she thinking?

Oh, Jacob Wilder, how I want to touch you.

He smiled, then immediately felt guilty for snooping. But he was glad he had. How exactly did she want to touch him?

"Have you worked in the tweed shop long?" he asked setting the basket of bread on the table. He wanted to know everything about her.

"About a year," she told him. "Before that, I was at University and before that I worked at the distillery."

"And you've been composing music between it all." He smiled, marveling at her.

"Yes."

"For a dream."

She looked up at him, her eyes wide with uncertainty. "Am I a fool?"

"No." He shook his head and smiled at her. She was better than fire, than flight. But he didn't tell her that.

He barely wanted to tell himself.

"Okay, ready to meet the band?"

Jacob looked up at Graham coming from the kitchen with Ivy in hot pursuit. "Sure, but is the band ready for River's music?" He winked at her as he stood up, but the moment he turned from her, his smile faded. A better question would be, was *he* ready for it?

CHAPTER ELEVEN

J ACOB WALKED ALONG the edge of the low cliff above the loch, alone in the dark. He didn't need moonlight to see the gulls roused from their nests in the rocks. He could hear other critters scurrying around him, a waterfall nearby, the wind winding around the mountains. River was right. It was musical.

He'd left her several hours ago, after spending the evening with her in a barn lit cozily by strings of lights. Being near her had almost been too distracting. If not for the amp a few inches away blasting her music into his eardrums, he wouldn't have been able to keep his thoughts off how she looked in the soft ambience, a crease marring her brow, one end of her bottom lip clenched between her teeth. She was worried at how her composition sounded mixed with the band's metal influence.

He'd spent three hours working with Graham and the band on softening certain pitches and building the crescendo with shorter, harder chords. He knew how she'd meant for the piece to sound, what inspired her to compose it. But he also didn't want the band to sacrifice their personal sound. No one rejected his ideas and, after some work, they had created something both River and the band were happy with.

River had been grateful. Thanks to a slight, subtle probe, he'd discovered that she wanted to throw her arms around his neck and hug him.

Hell, he was glad she hadn't done it. After playing her music all night, Drakkon was close. Jacob would hold back his fangs, his scales, his wings, but he wasn't sure he could leash his desire for her once Drakkon was involved. He would never hurt her. Never. He wanted to mold her to him, take her in his hands, with his mouth...these weren't things he'd ever felt before, but he'd never had to deny himself. It wouldn't have been so difficult if he didn't want to be around River every moment, if he didn't enjoy their time together so much.

He was changing, no longer the carefree bad boy from his pre-Drakkon days. He cared about River. He'd cared about her the moment he first looked into her eyes and saw the fight for her courage and composure amidst the terror of being eaten. Spending time with her inside his head and out of it, proved her resilience. She tended her father's cattle, walked to work and back home each day to cook and tend to her family, and kept her dream alive by composing beautiful music. He didn't know what kind of men she was used to in the past—the fool Colin might have hurt her, but she was an innocent when it came to love, as he was. And it was that purity—the most highly valued treasure to Drakkon—that called to him so strongly.

He'd had to leave her earlier, for the good of them both. Wanting to be the first and only man she ever loved was unfair and cruel, knowing what he knew.

He'd refused her offer to spend the night on the sofa instead of walking all the way back to Tarbert.

But he hadn't gone back to Tarbert. Instead, he'd lingered about the outside of the house for an hour or two, watching the sky—and the light in River's bedroom window go out.

She hadn't tried to contact Drakkon again. Jacob wasn't sure how he felt about it. He felt bad for not answering when she'd called. What was this hold River had over him? Was it a hold on his Drakkon heart...or his human heart? Or both?

He'd stopped trying to talk himself into leaving. He wasn't going anywhere. Not yet. Every time he thought about going, thoughts of her pulled him back, as if she held him tethered by unseen chains.

He had to leave Harris eventually. Even if he wasn't immortal—and a liar, they wanted different things. She wanted more than this quiet life. It was the longing he'd seen in her eyes when they'd met in the shop. Her music was her dream, the thing that gave her hope. He could make it happen for her. He knew enough people in the industry. He wanted to help her, but it meant going back into the world as Jacob White and risking being found by The Bane.

He wanted peace and quiet. He didn't want to live in big cities anymore, living on the run, being deafened by city sounds and poisoned by exhaust and pollution. He wanted...this.

But this life couldn't be his. Not without heartbreak. He'd done just fine all these years not relying on, or even considering his heart.

Hadn't he?

What was the empty hole in his life that nothing could fill? He'd thought it was flying, but even in flight it followed him. He hadn't felt it today—with her—with her family.

He looked up at the sky. Pre-dusk was approaching. The blue hour. Would he fly? It disgusted and scared him that, presently, he had no desire to be Drakkon. Would he let her stop him?

He watched the sky change, felt the stars pulling him, beckoning. He looked toward the water and then back in the direction of the house. No one was there.

His dream awaited. He pulled off his jacket and set it down on the rocks with his backpack. Flight was the instinct that drove him, not passion, not loneliness. He might have recently been turned, but Drakkon had always existed inside him. He undressed until he stood naked over the loch, then he dove into the water. He swam as far as he could and kept Drakkon clear in his mind. He wanted to shed his freezing skin, his heavy bones. He wanted to fly.

He felt his body start to change, beginning with the cold water no longer feeling cold. He concentrated on the fading stars and exploded out of the waves, sheets of water spilling off his great white wings.

RIVER ROSE WITH the sun, after getting two hours of sleep. She'd been up all night writing music, driven by a muse made of flesh, not scales. Jacob had easily fit into their family dinner, patiently answering everyone's questions. Her father liked him, but she'd expected that. Ivy had always been the hard one to win over, but she seemed to like him, too. Graham and the lads from the band certainly liked him. Who wouldn't? He was like looking at a star…the twinkling kind.

She sighed as his face crossed her mind; the angles of his high cheekbones and square, strong jaw against the dangling lights while he sat on a stool and taught the guys how to play her song. She could have fallen in love with him then and there. Any woman with blood in her veins would have. River thought she might have, especially when he pulled eight hundred dollars from his backpack, bought one of the band's acoustic guitars and handed it to her. She thought she'd loved Colin, but what she was beginning to feel for Jacob went deeper, to the pit of her guts.

She set out for Tarbert, though it was only to let Margery know she was calling out sick. She needed sleep. Unfortunately, there wasn't any cell phone connection in her village so she'd have to go to work to get the day off. She didn't mind. She wanted to stop off at the distillery, which *did* have WiFi, and do a little investigating on the Internet about Jacob Wilder.

She didn't know him. If he were just a popular musician, she wouldn't have been surprised to discover that he'd sought the limelight to avoid intimacy. The poor guy never had a family. No stable environment. He'd never formed attachments and probably thought he didn't need them. Easy. She could deal with that for however long he was staying.

It was his involvement with dragons that she had uncertainties about. It made her see things that were impossible, like the way his smoldering eyes sometimes looked at her the same way Drakkon's had when it had awakened from its slumber that early spring morning. Or hear something similar in the way he spoke her name. It was all so crazy and it swathed Jacob in mystery and made him even more irresistible. But she needed to keep a clear head and move with caution. If he was just a nice guy—with a sexy, slanted smile and killer eyes—and she really didn't mean anything to him and never would, then she didn't want to start anything.

But he made it difficult.

She was still thinking of him when a flash of light shimmered across the sky beyond the loch. Lightning? White clouds billowed across the sky, not gray. Drakkon?

Her heart leaped within. *Drakkon? Where are you?* She ran along the edge of the loch and spread her eyes over the sky. When her foot kicked something soft, she stopped and looked down.

A pile of clothes and a backpack rested at her feet. They were Jacob's. She looked out across the water. What the hell was he doing here, and in the loch? She reached down and picked up his shirt and held it to her nose.

Is the hunter still hanging around?

Drakkon. She raised her gaze from Jacob's shirt.

Yes, he's here. Is that why you're staying away?

What if it was? Would you send him away?

No.

You say that without hesitation, River.

I like him, she told him, a part of her wishing that he was Jacob and now he knew without her having to tell him face to face. She didn't want to like him, or anyone. She wanted to keep her heart safely in its place, where it could never be abandoned again.

Silence reigned for a few seconds that felt eternal. What was he thinking? *Where are you, Drakkon? Are you close by? Will I ever see you again?*

You might.

Her eye caught movement on the water. Jacob. He swam out of the thin morning mist that covered the surface like a fantasy coming to life. She momentarily forgot about Drakkon and watched Jacob's sleek body pushing closer. How far out had he been? Was he naked? Her eyes darted to his clothes...his knickers. Her face went hot. She spun around, keeping her back to him when he reached the rock and began pulling himself up.

She'd forgotten she stood over his clothes until he came to stand just behind her. She could hear his breath and feel his leashed energy.

"Did I frighten you?" His thick baritone along her ear made her kneecaps sizzle.

"No," she said without turning. "What are you doing out here?"

"Having a swim," he said, moving around behind her. "You?"

"I...I...ehm..." Should she tell him that she thought she saw Drakkon—or lightning? That she'd just spoken with the White in her head? What would Jacob say? Yes, River, I know. It was me. Or, would he demand to know everything and try to use her to catch Drakkon?

"You can turn around now," he suggested.

She obeyed his sorcerer's chant. She shouldn't have. He stood shirtless and glistening beneath the morning sun. His hair hung loose to his shoulders, like a wilted halo, dripping water down his sculpted arms, his chest, his long, lean six-pack abs. He'd exchanged his jeans for a pair of looser-fitting, tan, drawstring trousers that rode low on his hips.

River bit her lip and looked up into his sunlit eyes eclipsed by his hair. He was temptation incarnate. Exactly the kind of guy she should steer clear of; gorgeous, trouble, baggage.

"Did you sleep well?"

She nodded. He was too dangerous. He tempted her to do too many things, like give up her body and her heart—lick a droplet of water off his shoulder or...lower. "Jacob?" she managed between two shallow breaths.

He dipped his head slightly so he could get a deeper look into her eyes. "Yes?"

How in the world could a simple word make her go weak and willing? Or was it the way he looked at her like he would have given her anything she asked. "Can you put on a shirt? I need to stay focused."

He laughed the same way he spoke, deep and low, resonating through her blood.

She watched him bend to his backpack and pull out a black sweater. He put it on, but it didn't help. The black only served to accentuate the opposite. The neckline of the slightly oversized sweater was a little tattered and worn around the cuffs. He put his jacket and boots in the bag and left his feet bare. He looked comfortable and at ease with himself, and so attractive it made her lightheaded.

"Better?" He held out his arms and she did everything she could not to throw herself into them. What would she find there? Passion and comfort, or insincerity and false affection that wouldn't last an hour after he left?

"River, I understand that Colin hurt you—"

"What?" she asked, stepping away. "What does that have to do with anything?"

"It's why you're cautious."

She stared into his eyes. Did she just hear him right? What did he know about Colin and her insecurities? Colin was the first and only guy she'd ever slept with, who'd told her he loved her, and then left.

How did Jacob seem to know all her secrets and desires? Why did he feel so familiar?

She remembered what Drakkon had told her. He could read her thoughts. It was how he'd known her name.

Her blood pulsed through her veins. She had to command each breath. Was Jacob reading her thoughts? Was he—

"Ivy told me Colin was an asshole," Jacob's audible voice broke through her thoughts. He spoke on a low rumble, tender and hypnotic. "Don't be angry with her, though. She spoke from love and concern for you."

River thought about it for a minute. Ivy had told him. She wasn't going crazy then. "Still," she told him in a soft voice and then turned away. "My caution has more to do with you than with Colin. I have too many questions about you and the more I talk to you, the more I have."

She began walking back toward the road. Jacob followed her, still barefoot. He tossed his backpack over his shoulder and raked his fingers through his wet hair, dragging it over his forehead. "You're driving me mad. Is that enough to know?"

His confession was so unexpected that she turned to him and laughed. "That's a terrible thing to say!"

He creased his brow. "Why?"

"How am I driving you mad?"

"You're always in my thoughts."

She stopped again and faced him. Was he always so disarming? Was it genuine? Was he truly addled by her? What if he was? What did it mean?

"What do you think about?" she asked.

His slow, seductive smile told her all she wanted to know, but he told her anyway. "Kissing you." He took a step closer. His hair fell back around his eyes when he dipped his head to look at her. "Touching you." He lifted his fingers to her jaw but barely touched her.

She wanted him to. She wanted him to reach out for her and pull her in close, take her in his arms and kiss her socks off.

He traced his knuckles over her cheek and then swept his hand behind her nape. He used little effort to pull her closer to him, his gaze hovering above her, burning on her parted lips, her breath captured by his. The tips of her breasts pushed against him and, for a moment, he looked about to ravish her completely. He drifted back an inch, teasing her, testing his limits, then returned, poised at the edge of her mouth.

Instead of kissing her, he sighed, muttered an oath, and pulled back. "River, there's something you should know."

Her head cleared and she reached out for him. "What is it?"

"I'm..." He began and then stopped again. He took her hand and held it between them. "Your dragon's name isn't Drakkon."

How did he know what she called the White? Her stomach clenched in a knot that nearly doubled her over. "What is it then?"

It's Jacob. Jacob White.

CHAPTER TWELVE

RIVER PULLED HER hand from his and took a step back. Did she just hear Jacob in her head? This couldn't be—he couldn't be—she thought seeing a real dragon was the most incredible, unbelievable thing that could ever happen to her. But this was bigger. This was even harder to believe.

Jacob?

"Yes, River," he answered out loud, proving he was reading her thoughts.

Her heart faltered. Reading her thoughts—all this time.

"I should have told you—"

"You're Drakkon? But…how? How can you…?"

Oh, this was too much. Her crazy suspicions had been correct. Jacob was Drakkon. Dear God, she was falling for a dragon! And she *was* falling for him! How could she not? He cared about her music. He cared enough to patiently sit with Graham's band for three hours, helping them understand her piece.

He'd understood it because it was about him.

He was Drakkon. What did it mean? Should she run for her life or thrill at the thought of having a dragon-shifter in her life?

"Then you're not a hunter?" Oh, hell, she didn't want that to be her first question. Everything had obviously been a lie. Was the Red a lie, too? Had Drak—Jacob killed her cattle?

"Let's walk or find somewhere to sit," he offered reaching for her arm. "I'll tell you everything."

She pushed his hand away. "Are you really a dragon, Jacob?" It was almost too outlandish to utter. "Did you eat my father's cattle?"

"We're called Drakkon," he corrected. "And no, I didn't. The Red is real."

Was the Red a man, too? Could she have seen him before—in the shop, at University? He could be anywhere. "So what, there's a whole race of you out there? Dragon-shifters?" She held her palms to her head before she spun back around in the direction of the road. "No, seriously, this isn't happening."

He came up beside her. His voice was so low she hardly heard him. "It is."

If it was, there was too much to consider. She was glad he hadn't kissed her. "Then you've been eavesdropping on my private thoughts, playing some kind of game—"

No, he came barreling inside her head. *I didn't know how to tell you.*

Stop it! Get out of my head!

"No one is supposed to know," he said aloud. "I'll probably get into trouble for telling you."

"Get in trouble with whom?" she asked incredulously, storming toward Tarbert. "Dragon hunters who don't exist?"

"They do exist," he insisted. "The Bane is real."

She recoiled, thinking of men without mercy hunting Jacob. There was so much she didn't know. Her head was spinning in a hundred different directions. "Are they after you?"

He shook his head. "They don't know I'm Drakkon."

"How do you know that?"

"Because I work for them. I'm one of them. Though I've never hunted Drakkon."

River closed her eyes and was tempted to stop and punch him for bringing so much confusion into her life.

"Everything I told you so far is true, River." His damned silky voice sounded in her ears. "I just haven't told you everything."

She turned to look at him as the road swung left and they followed the footpath to Urgha. No wonder he was so beautiful and breathtaking. He was Drakkon. How? How was he a dragon? "I don't think I want to know."

"Okay," he said quietly, keeping pace.

They walked on in silence for a little longer. River was thankful that he didn't try to speak to her in her head, but the silence was driving her crazy. What was going to happen now? He was a dragon! "There can't be anymore listening in," she said, glancing at him. "I need a place to hide from you."

"Why?"

"What do you mean, why?" She laughed a little but she felt like crying. Had she really fallen for a guy who could turn into a dragon? A guy who knew what she was thinking all the time and didn't respect her space? "Everyone needs their own private thoughts, Jacob. Even you."

He nodded and crossed his wrists behind his back. "I'll do my best. It'll be difficult though. I like your thoughts."

He didn't look at her while he spoke but kept his eyes toward the small bridge coming up in the distance, and still he captivated her. She blushed trying to recall some of her thoughts he might have been privy to. "I'm sure you do like them, since we just met and you've been nothing but charming. Listen in after some time and you might not like it so much."

"If you don't hate me right now," he said, glancing at her from beneath his brow, mesmerizing her with the slightest movement of his tongue against the inside of his cheek. "I don't think you will after 'some time'."

He had every reason to be cocky about it, but he wasn't. He was uncomfortable. He looked out of his element. How was that possible? Surely, there had been plenty of women in his life. "I don't hate you," she said softly, angry with herself for falling under his spell. "But I don't trust you. You lied to me and you didn't keep your promise about not reading my mind."

"I'm trying to remedy those things right now," he pointed out. "Your trust has value to me."

"Why?" she couldn't help but ask.

"I told you, River, I like you."

"Me and how many others?" she scoffed lightly.

His gaze burned through her, heating her flesh, her blood. "Just you."

Just her? Her mouth betrayed her and she smiled like some adoring fan. What was she doing? She'd sworn to herself never to be swayed by a guy's looks again. Colin was devilishly handsome but, in the end, there was no substance. Jacob, on the other hand...what? What had he done besides promise her things and keep huge secrets? Huge.

And one of the promises he'd made, not to read her thoughts, he hadn't kept.

She looked away and stopped smiling. "I feel like I know you less than I did yesterday. I don't understand how any of this is possible. Or how you can be a dragon *and* a dragon hunter? I don't even know if I believe that you're Drakkon. I don't know what to believe."

"I am Drakkon."

The hint of arrogance in his voice drew her gaze back to him. With his loose, white-gold hair drying in the breeze and flowing off his broad shoulders and his strong, angular profile, she could easily believe he was the majestic white dragon she'd seen.

"Prove it."

He turned his head and crooked his mouth at her. "It's too risky. I don't know how dangerous I am."

"How can you not know?"

"Because I'm new at this. At being Drakkon. I don't know the extent of my desire."

She stopped for a moment and turned to him, her wry smile belying the curiosity in her eyes. "What do you mean, you're new at being Drakkon? You weren't born this way? Someone turned you?"

He nodded, squinting in the sun. "It's a long story, River."

She stepped off the side of the road and sat down on a small bench for tourists overlooking the loch.

"I have time."

He smiled down at her and drew both hands through his hair. "Okay then. Do I have your word never to repeat this to anyone?"

When she agreed, he sat next to her and started at the beginning.

JACOB'S INTENTION WASN'T to tell River everything. She already knew more about him than anyone else. He realized with frightening clarity that he wanted her to know him…all of him. He was losing his heart to her and he had no idea what to do about it. It scared the hell out of him for more reasons than he wanted to think about, and was more thrilling than the first time he changed back into a man while flying. It was new and pure and his heart couldn't help but want more of it.

Confessing to her was easier than he'd expected, more liberating than anything he'd ever dreamed. He'd been living behind a cavalier mask, learning to smile for the camera, disconnected from a world that didn't know him and never would.

And then he'd seen her—the first human through his Drakkon eyes, standing tall against him like some mythical warrior goddess. The first, besides Helena and Garion, to speak in his thoughts.

He knew he was in trouble but he'd been in trouble before. Still, his heart had never been involved. He'd never been half-Drakkon. He was unfamiliar with the emotions roiling up inside him, like the need to possess her, to be near her, the desire to hold her, kiss her, make her his. Since returning to Harris, he'd found himself wanting to do things to make her happy. He wouldn't read her thoughts again unless she allowed it. He'd broken her trust and he wanted to gain it back.

So he told her his secrets.

She listened intently, taking in every word, stopping him for clarity about Garion's power and about The Bane a few times.

"Your father almost singlehandedly annihilated the entire Drakkon race."

"Almost," he agreed.

"Do you remember him?"

Jacob shook his head and set his eyes on the loch. "He wanted to kill Garion for his essence and use it to raise an army of Drakkon against mankind. He was a traitor to both his races. I take no pride that his blood flows through my veins. It's a good thing Marrkiya killed him."

"Marrkiya changed my father's life, mine and Ivy's, too."

Her voice saturated him like mist from the clouds. He turned to look at her. He was falling in love with her face and all its little nuances; her intelligent, expressive eyes, her small, pert nose, and the beguiling contour of her jaw. She smiled. His gaze dipped to her mouth.

"It made us stronger. Closer."

"I'm glad," he told her. He admired her for seeing the good in something that cost her family so much. "You're very courageous, River."

"No—" she said, shaking her head.

"Yes, you are. You're the bravest women I've ever met. The way you faced me and made your deal, and not just for yourself but for your village. Most hu—people have died of fright."

"You don't know me," she whispered.

"I do," he whispered back and smiled when she looked at him.

"You don't know that I'm a coward when it comes to leaving here for good, or that the people I made the deal for haunt my memories with things they said or did to my father."

"Despite what they did, they're your friends...even family, or else you wouldn't have stood up for them."

"Yes," she agreed.

"You've forgiven them, River. There's nothing holding you back now."

Her smile was more radiant than a thousand sunrises. "Thank you, Jacob."

He moved in closer and she laughed softly, filling his ears with music, and moved out of his reach. "Tell me more about you," she said, stopping his advance.

He would be patient.

"Seeing a dragon burn your home and your family must have been life changing."

"I never blamed him for raining fire on The Bane that night. Garion was a kid, too, and The Bane had just killed his first foster father, and two of his friends that he'd altered. They were children. My relatives burned them. *That* was when my life changed. When I knew that I sympathized with the Drakkon race. I couldn't let anyone know. I couldn't tell them that I'd always felt the desire to fly. They wouldn't have understood."

"So you grew up never belonging anywhere," she said softly, her eyes wide and glistening like the summer sea, "or to anyone."

He softened his smile on her. After all this, there was still compassion in her eyes for him. "I did all right for the most part," he reassured her softly. "I made my own way."

He told her about his life—things he'd never told anyone before her, like the meanings behind many of his songs, and why he wrote them.

"I grew up defiant and…" He looked away from her and laughed a little at himself, at things he hadn't realized until now. "…basically pissed off at life. I had this blood in my veins from my father that made me more than what I was and I couldn't grab hold of it. I longed to fly. I hated Drakkon for emblazoning its instincts on my soul, and mankind for keeping them from me. The anger landed me in detention facilities a few times but, eventually, I learned to shut it all off. When the Elders came to me with an offer to erase my criminal record if I rejoined The Bane, I agreed." He glanced up at her from beneath his brows. "Now, everything has changed."

She lifted her fingers to a lock of hair at his temple to brush it back. He tilted his face toward her touch and closed his eyes as he kissed her palm.

"Your dreams have come true."

He opened his eyes at the sound of her tender voice and looked into the blue fathoms of her gaze. "Yes, they have." But he was here with her. Should he tell her that she'd stepped into his path and now the sky didn't feel as important? He wasn't sure he wanted to voice *that* yet.

She lowered her hand from his face but he clasped it in his and stood up.

"We should be moving on. You're going to be late for work."

She didn't pull her hand away and he suspected, without reading her thoughts, that she was feeling the same electrical charge as he was, coursing through her blood. He glanced at her again and smiled. Was her heart also filled to bursting with warmth and satisfaction?

She asked him more questions on the way to Tarbert, questions about Helena, the Elders, The Bane, and Jeremy the Red. He told her what she wanted to know.

The only thing he didn't tell her was that he was immortal.

He didn't know how he was going to tell her that.

Jacob, another voice broke through his head, *we're here.*

Helena. He gritted his teeth and slid his gaze to River, who was oblivious to his conversation. What the hell was he going to tell them about her? *What do you mean you're here?* He didn't know why he looked up. They wouldn't have flown here. *You were supposed to give me a week.*

Jacob, there's another Drakkon in the sky and we still can't find him on Garion's Onyx. We don't have a week. Frankly, I'm surprised you're not taking this more seriously.

"Jacob?" River tugged on his hand, bringing him to a halt, pulling his gaze to her. "What's wrong?"

Now, where are you? His sister continued. *Is it densely populated? Is there a place to stay while we plan this thing out?*

"It's my sister," he told River, casting his sister's voice to the back of his mind. "She's talking to me, which means she's in range. She and Garion are here."

Her eyes opened wider and, like him, she looked up. He reached out and spread his fingers over the bottom of her tilted chin, down her neck.

At his touch, she lowered her gaze to his. He stepped closer.

"Don't be afraid," he whispered.

"I'm not."

He smiled, staring into her eyes. He should have remembered how this woman kicked fear in the face. But this was more than fear. This was Drakkon. The Red was flying around somewhere—maybe close. They needed to stop it.

Jacob told his sister where he would be and then, before he broke their connection, he told her he wasn't leaving.

Not yet.

CHAPTER THIRTEEN

R IVER DIDN'T HAVE enough time to process everything Jacob had told her while they waited for the ferry to dock. She was about to meet, quite literally, the father of dragons—the new kind, at least. The kind that could change at will. She was about to meet a man who'd been hatched. She felt a little queasy.

"Will he be able to read my thoughts?" she turned to ask Jacob, standing beside her.

"I'm going to ask him not to," he said on a low, rumbling murmur.

"And if he refuses?"

"He won't."

He sounded sure, but she didn't want another man in her head finding out things about her without her permission. "Is there some kind of Drakkon law or code he has to follow if you ask?"

He lowered his gaze and his voice. "Something like that."

She almost didn't hear him. What was he trying to hide? "Something like what, Jacob?"

"If I—ehm—" He lifted his eyes to hers and, in them, she saw both the Drakkon, hungry for her—and the man, unsure if she was going to hit him. "—claim possession of you."

She smiled and then laughed a little. "You realize how barbaric and ancient that sounds, right?"

He hooked one corner of his mouth at her.

Right, she conceded. Dragons.

She watched the people departing the ferry. There were about a dozen—tourists here for the day. Most of them were looking behind them at the couple leaving last.

River didn't know what she'd expected to see when Jacob had told her about the Gold. How does one measure a Drakkon king by human standards? Even with her imagination, she would have fallen short if she tried. Garbed in the splendor of the sun, his hair lit like a gilded gold crown, Garion Gold looked more like a god than a king. His clothes were expensive and cut well to fit his tall, muscular physique. He carried three large backpacks on his broad shoulders and a smaller carrier in his hand.

His wife was no less beautiful and regal with wide, deep blue eyes and a mantle of pearly white hair shot through with bolts of gold piled atop her head in a thick bun. She wore a cable-knit sweater, a shade lighter than her eyes, snug-fitting jeans, and hiking boots.

"She doesn't look like the kind of woman who can be possessed," River leaned in to tell Jacob, keeping her eyes on the confident-looking woman on her way toward them.

"They're life mates," Jacob told her. "They possess each other with equal measure."

She looked up at him, forgetting his family. "Life mates?"

Jacob suddenly went stiff. "Sorry. Helena." He pointed to his head to indicate his sister was speaking to him. River narrowed her eyes and didn't push it when he didn't explain. Life mates, huh? It didn't sound like something a guy who'd never had attachments would take kindly to. She guessed there were some things about being a Drakkon that, for Jacob, weren't dreams come true. He clearly wasn't comfortable with commitment. How long would he stay with her before he left?

The closer his sister and her husband grew, the harder it become to focus on anything else but them. How could they ever stay hidden from The Bane when they stood out like the sun and the stars in a fog? They appeared as surprised by her presence as she was of theirs.

You didn't tell them about me.

Jacob turned to her, surprised to hear her in his head. *I didn't know what to tell them.*

"Jake!" his sister reached them and kissed him on the cheek. "It's good to see you." She pinched her fingers on the tattered neckline of his sweater and tugged at it. "Though you look like a penniless drifter."

Without skipping a beat or giving her husband a chance to speak—though by the way he was staring at Jacob, it appeared he might already be engaged in another conversation—she turned her striking smile on River. For an uneasy moment, she stared into River's eyes as if she might know her.

"Helena Gold." She made a half-turn. "My husband, Garion."

Garion turned his topaz-colored eyes on River and her knees went a little weak. This tower of flames before her had power beyond compare. If not for Jacob, no man would compare. She heard a meow and looked at the carrier in his hand. A little, white Persian cat pulled his attention.

"And you are?" Helena asked her.

For a moment, River was too lost in their radiance to remember her name. They were Drakkons. She wondered what they looked like in scales and spikes. Drakkons with a cat. "I'm River..." she said in a low voice. "River Wray."

Helena Gold flicked her sharp gaze to her brother. "You told her."

River scowled at her. How did she know that? Had she just read River's thoughts?

"I would appreciate it if you wouldn't do that," River said in a soft voice, pulling Helena's attention back to her. She'd stand her ground, but Helena Gold would be intimidating even if she wasn't a Drakkon.

She didn't ask River what she was talking about. She knew. She lifted her elegant brow and was about to say something when she stopped and tilted her head in her husband's direction.

They were communicating in private, coming to conclusions about her that she couldn't defend.

She doesn't like me. River aimed at Jacob.

She likes strength, and you have it. She likes you.

River cast him a slight smile and then continued waiting.

They do this to me all the time. Jacob's voice came softly to her head. *It's rude.*

He nodded, and his sister noticed.

They know we're talking.

Good. There was satisfaction in giving them a taste of their own medicine.

She felt Jacob's eyes on her and turned. They shared a smile. For River though, it was so much more than that. Did sharing thoughts bond one to another person in a deeper, more intimate way?

"Jacob," his sister interrupted, "is what you told Garion true?"

What? River blinked. What had Jacob told him?

"Yes, I claim possession of her," Jacob provided, keeping his eyes on his sister and not on River. "I've asked him not to probe her."

"Jake," his sister expelled a short laugh. "You're not—"

River cleared her throat. "Excuse me, I'm not his possession."

"You are to him." Garion said, quieting the birds in the air. His voice rumbled like the foundation beneath a mountain. He smiled and River wasn't sure if he smiled at her or because the cat he'd set free had just leaped onto his shoulder. "In his telling of us, did he mention Drakkon treasures?"

She shook her head and glanced at Jacob. "Treasure?"

"It can be anything," the Gold king told her, touching his nose to the white ball of fluff snuggling in the crook of his neck.

"Like a cat," his wife said beside him.

"Or a woman." Garion pulled her close and smiled into her eyes as if she were the most priceless of treasures.

"You know," Jacob interrupted, "I think I like it better when you keep it to yourselves."

Garion, the bigger of the two, laughed and shot his hand out to give Jacob a playful shove.

Jacob smacked it away with a laugh of his own then reached up to pet the cat. "Come on. I'll take you to the B&B. Carina's freezing."

River detoured to the shop to let Margery know she wouldn't be coming in, then hurried back to the B&B. She met Jacob on the way. He was alone, walking toward her. His hair was tied back once again. "Is something wrong?" she asked when they reached each other on the narrow road.

"No." He lifted a curious brow at her. "Why?"

"I said I'd meet you at the B&B. What are you doing here?"

"I wanted to ask you something."

She wondered if it was the husky timbre of his voice or the warm caress of his gaze that melted her resolve and made her belly flip and her skin feel hot.

"Yes?"

A playful smile curled his mouth. "Did you miss me?"

She felt her cheeks go up in flames and lowered her gaze to keep him from seeing the truth in her eyes. "I saw you less than ten minutes ago."

He laughed. "All right."

"What?" She looked up and couldn't help but laugh with him. "How am I supposed to answer that?"

"Honestly," he replied a bit more soberly.

She shook her head in mock amazement at him. "Sometimes, it's like you're newer at this than I am."

"I am."

She expected him to laugh at her preposterous suggestion. How could he possibly be inexperienced at courting? His flirtations were disarming and genuinely innocent, making his natural charm that much more beguiling. Could he have kept his heart from everyone until…until now? Just as she had? She stared at him, searching his eyes, his face for the truth.

Like a breeze across her mind, he let her into his thoughts. She felt his confusion and hesitation to dive into unchartered waters. She understood that a part of him *was* new and unfamiliar. It was his heart. She'd somehow gained access to it where none had before. She felt his affection for her like a warm cloak covering her, desire that turned the cloak to fire. She fought to keep her heart intact. He was a dragon. It might be romantic in a book, but this was real life. She didn't know anything about dragons! How could this ever work?

"Fine," she said, turning for the B&B, yanking herself from his thoughts, her heart pounding hard in her chest. "I missed you. Are you happy now?"

He caught up to her quickly and leaned in to say softly against her ear, "Yes, River, now I am."

She turned her face, wanting to see in his eyes what she heard in his voice. Her lips brushed along his jaw. Something electric coursed through her blood and tempted her to grab fistfuls of his hair and drag his mouth to hers.

"Jake!" His sister's voice broke through the pounding drumbeats. She was running toward them.

The wind had stopped. The birds had gone silent. River's heart slowed as she halted her breath. This had happened before when—

From up over the cliff side, it rose on twenty-plus foot, slow-flapping wings the color of blood. In the stillness, the sound of his wings moving the air was amplified. It was bulkier, more muscular than the graceful beauty of the White. It must have been flying low above the surface of the loch. No one had seen it until it was too late— and directly in their path.

River looked into its gaping mouth for an instant before Jacob closed his arms around her and leaped out of the way, narrowly escaping the red dragon's snapping jaws. They landed in the dirt but Jacob rose up instantly and pulled off his shirt.

"Jake!" his sister shouted as the dragon flew away and the people who'd come out of their businesses to see the dragon screamed. "Not here!"

But it was too late. River watched his trousers tear away and his flesh harden into scales. She lifted her head as he rose high above her, his long, muscular neck stretching toward the sky.

Drakkon! It was Drakkon! Believing Jacob was Drakkon was one thing. Seeing him was another thing altogether. He hadn't left her. He'd been with her all this time, watching over her, opening his heart to her. His size and sheer pearly radiance stole her breath away. His limbs were as thick as a dozen tree trunks, with golden-tipped, teardrop scales overlapping to create thick armor. He breathed and sunlight ricocheted off the iridescent hues of his scales. He lowered his large, spiked head and set his fiery blue gaze on her. Jacob.

Jacob.

Silence answered her as he swung his head toward the direction the Red had just taken. He exhaled and smoke blew from his nostrils. He swished his spade-tipped tail and unfurled his wings. One mighty flap sent dirt and pebbles everywhere and lifted him off the ground, and the second gave him flight.

Someone was screaming. Was it her? This was all really happening. A Drakkon had almost eaten her and Jacob!

She stood up and looked for Helena and Garion. They were gone. About twenty people stood around her, looking dazed and horrified. What should she do? She didn't realize she was shaking until she leaned down to pick up Jacob's backpack. They would have been gone in an instant if not for him. Terror crept up her spine as she looked around at the faces staring back at her. They'd seen the Drakkons.

They'd seen Jacob.

She spotted Margery stepping in front of the shop and Ivy running toward her from the distillery. Who would the dragon try to eat next?

Jacob?

Go home, River, she heard him. *Get your family and go to the barn. Wait for us there. Leave clothes for us outside. My backpack should be near you.*

I have it. Jacob—

"River!" Ivy screamed, reaching her. She threw her arms around her sister. "River, I thought that thing had eaten you! It was a dragon! It tried to eat you!" She held River tight and cried into her sweater. "Then...then I saw you. Oh, thank God, I saw you...and Jacob."

"Come, Ivy, we have to go."

"River," her sister stopped her. Then she wiped her eyes. "Da was right. He's been right all this time. There *are* dragons!"

"Are you all right, Miss?"

River turned to the frantic voice of a man she didn't know. A tourist.

"Yes," she assured, still a little disheveled. "I'm fine, thank you."

"I never saw anything like it," he said. His eyes were wide, his lips pale. "I'm here from California with my wife." He pointed into the small crowd. "We're sightseeing. Never expected to see that."

River didn't know what to say. She needed to go, and take Ivy with her.

"I don't know what I saw." She choked out a laugh. "It happened so fast."

He smiled and something about the heat in his dark gaze stopped her from moving. He was a stocky man, mid-twenties, his head shaved bald beneath a thin, woolen cap. He wore a tweed sweater and baggy jeans. He had one arm. "Too bad I didn't get a picture."

She nodded and pushed Ivy on her way. "We should probably get off the road."

"Keep your eyes open," the man called out as she and Ivy left. "That monster could be anywhere."

CHAPTER FOURTEEN

WHERE IS HE! Jacob shouted in his head as he flew northeast with nothing but empty clouds in his wide scope of vision.

He disappeared, Helena's voice answered from the southern sky. *How could he have disappeared right under our noses?*

The same way he arrived out of nowhere, Garion's voice joined theirs, turning Jacob's blood cold. *He altered. He must have done it almost immediately after the attack. We can't find him because we're looking for Drakkon.*

The Red was walking. If he'd changed immediately then he was likely closer to River than Jacob wanted him to be.

With a stroke of his mighty tail, he changed course and flew toward Tarbert.

Jeremy! He sent out to the four winds, hoping the Red was listening. *You tried to snap her up in your jaws. I'm going to kill you for that.*

Jacob White, I wish I could say this was a surprise, a thick, raspy voice answered a moment later. *I knew Garion would change you once your sister got her claws into him. How is Helena, by the way? Such a pretty little morsel.*

Jacob opened his thoughts to Garion so he could listen in. *What are you doing here, Red?* he demanded. *How are you alive?*

I need a mate. I'm here for Garion's blood.

Garion's voice came like thunder, momentarily rattling Jacob's thoughts. *Come and get it, Red.*

Hello, old friend, Red greeted. *I'm glad to know that you've finally come to your senses and agreed to alter more descendants. Jacob White is a fine example of your work. I look forward to seeing Helena—and your hot sister. Have you turned Ellie yet, big brother? May I?*

Jacob would help Garion kill this piece of shit. *Where are you?*

Don't worry, his voice raked across Jacob's thoughts. *I'm away from the girl with the pretty, red hair. I wasn't trying to eat her, but you. I didn't know she was yours until I spoke to her.*

Jacob's throat burned with a roaring fire. He beat his wings and rode the wind, severing contact with him.

River. His heart boomed in his ears, growing faster, louder with every second she didn't answer him. The Red was right, she was his. But she was more than a possession. She was his desire, his ache, the captor of his heart. *River, please—*

Jacob, what's wrong? Where are you?

He shifted the angle of his tail and flew toward Tarbert. *I'm coming. Did a man speak to you? Is he anywhere near you now?*

Yes, a man spoke to me. I don't see him around. He said he was a tourist and he saw you. How did you know he spoke to me?

What did he say to you?

He asked if I was okay, and...he creeped me out a little. He told me to keep my eyes open because the monster could be anywhere. Jacob, was he the Red?

Yes, he told her, almost there. *Forget the barn. Hide behind something until I get there.*

The slope.

Yes, his heart warmed at the thought of her, composed and strong in the midst of this.

We need clothes, Helena's voice broke the dreadful silence. *And please get Carina.*

Yes, I have her, River answered, sounding relieved by the change of subject. *And the clothes. I'm almost there. I have Ivy. Hurry.*

Jacob pulled his wings in close to his body and dove from the clouds above Tarbert. He saw River below, atop the hill, looking up, and Ivy pointing her phone at him. He stretched his wings and soared toward the vale. He kept his eyes on the sky and the earth, watching River and Ivy hurry down the back of the slope to deposit their clothes.

He landed with perfect ease a short distance from them and folded his wings over his back. River stared at him, much the same way she had the first time she'd seen him. Astounded, curious, in control of her emotions, except one. Her joy at seeing him hit him like a golden arrow to the heart.

It made him want to be a man. He felt himself altering. *Turn Ivy around.*

River did as he asked, slipping her own eyes back to him as he altered and walked toward his backpack naked.

He met her gaze and was about to smile when Ivy screamed.

It was Charlie Owens. Killed by the Red, most likely for his clothes and dumped here. Jacob pulled on his black jeans and tattered sweater and hurried to them. He took River under his arm, but Ivy pulled away from him.

She stared into his eyes, at the contours of his face, forgetting the dead body near her. "You're one of them." Disgust and then fear contorted her features when she looked behind him at the naked couple that had just landed. She turned her gaze to her sister's and gave her arm—looped through the handle of Carina's carrier—a tug. "No one is safe."

"These three will not hurt us," River reassured her.

"I want to protect you," Jacob added calmly.

Ivy didn't look convinced, but there was no time for that now. He heard Garion and Helena come up behind him and watched his brother-in-law, fully dressed, lean over the body.

"His neck is broken," he informed them. He looked up at his wife. "I just spoke to Ellie. She's going to stay low."

Helena nodded and stepped forward to take River's hand. "What did the man who spoke to you look like?"

"He was bald," River told her, handing Carina over to Garion.

"Did he have one arm or two?"

Jacob's gaze flicked to Garion's and then back to River. He had forgotten what could be possible. His pulse quickened.

"One."

River's answer caused the same reaction in all three Drakkon. They smiled, learning a little more about the essence that flowed through their veins. It didn't regenerate what was cut, or hacked, or bitten off. Jeremy's head it must be then. "We have to cut off his head," Garion told them. Jacob and Helena nodded. So did River.

They spread out and searched the ferry terminal and everywhere else in Tarbert. Jeremy Redmond was nowhere to be found.

"We need to keep them safe," Jacob told Garion an hour later, after his brother-in-law returned from the B&B with his Onyx and their bags. "I know a place on Skye—"

"Red knows we're here," Garion said. "He wants my blood. He'll be back. If we leave Harris, we just delay what we could get done now."

"Right," Jacob agreed. "But they're in harm's way here."

"Until we take down the Red," Helena reminded him, "they're not safe anywhere. No one is. His veiled threat about being anywhere is real. But we'll find him."

Jacob knew she was right, and if anyone could find a man, it was his sister. She'd found Marcus Aquara and Garion Gold. Before she fell in love, she'd dedicated her life to The Bane and hunting Drakkon.

"I don't want them here when he returns," he insisted. Jeremy was clearly a sneaky, clever bastard. He'd gotten close to River in both his forms. Jacob didn't want to take that chance again.

"They're safest with us," Garion said. "If you want to protect them, keep them close."

"You can all stay at my house," River offered and then turned to him. "I'm not leaving without you. I won't go."

He stepped closer to her and looked deep in her eyes. She had too much courage. Red was playing with them. Jeremy could have hurt her. The thought of it made him want to go on a fiery rampage. It also made him think about his days without her in them. Now or later. It was only going to get harder.

I can't believe you told her about us, Helena's voice sounded in his head after they started on the path back to Maraig, *or that you seem interested in someone for more than a night in bed. We have a lot to talk about, Brother.*

Jacob tossed her a scowl. *I wasn't that bad.* He knew he was. He just didn't want to be reminded of it.

Yes, you were. I see what attracts you to River, but it's hard to believe you've noticed.

I have.

Walking beside him and taking note of his scowl, River leaned in close. "What's she saying?"

He looked at her and thought about all the truths she'd accepted about him already. Should he push more right now or lie to her again? "She's seeing a side of me she's never seen before."

"Oh?" River tilted her face to his and broke down his scowl with the slightest of smiles. "What side is that?"

"Everything that was hidden before." He looked at her and smiled, baffled about how to explain himself or pinpoint any one part of him.

"So, why don't you two tell us how you met?"

Jacob flicked his icy gaze to his sister, who had hurried to catch up to them. "Maybe later."

"Are you an *Everbound* fan?" Helena ignored him and asked River.

"She's not a fan," Jacob said, holding up his palm. He knew she wouldn't stop until she leaned everything she wanted to know. He'd save her the trouble. "She came upon me while I slept in my new form. I spoke to her telepathically and we stayed in contact after I left Harris."

Ivy tossed River a disapproving look. "You knew what he was all this time?"

"No," River corrected her. "I didn't know the dragon was Jacob until this morning. I didn't tell you or Da about him because I'd made a deal with him not to tell anyone if he stayed away."

"You made a deal with him?" Helena asked, stunned. "With a Drakkon?"

"Yes, and I thought he broke his end of the bargain when my father's cattle were eaten." River finished the tale, leaving little out but the strong attraction and desire they felt toward each other.

Soon, Helena weaseled her way into Jacob's spot and curled her arm around River's. Jacob should be concerned about what his sister might say, but he wanted to speak with Ivy. With his nosey sister engaged in conversation and Garion keeping to the rear with his nose in his seeing Onyx, this was a good opportunity. He liked River's sister. She was honest and though she possessed a hard shell, she was vulnerable on the inside. He was also fairly certain that he was falling in love with her sister. He didn't want to be on Ivy's bad side if she might one day be a part of his family.

His family.

He thought of last night's dinner with the Wrays and Graham. He hoped for more of the same tonight, this time with Helena and Garion there as well. Had this been what he'd wanted all this time? A family?

He took up his steps beside her and shoved his hands into the front pockets of his jeans. "I'm sorry I lied to you, Ivy."

She didn't answer right away, making Jacob squirm. What more should he say? "I should have—"

"You don't have to do this, Jacob," she said, holding up her hands.

"I want to apologize to you. I'm not known to do it often, so please hear me out."

"What is there to say? Do you know what a dragon did to my life?" she asked sharply. "To my father's life?"

"No one believed what he saw," Jacob replied quietly. "I only know that."

She pulled the hood of her sweatshirt over her head and looked out over the loch. "That dragon robbed me and River of our mother, my father of his wife."

Jacob shook his head. She needed to come to terms with the truth or she would always hate what he was. "The dragon didn't take her, her unbelief and shame did."

She turned around and looked at him. Anger and sadness played across her features like a haunting song written on a dreary day.

"I'm sorry she left you," he said softly, "I know you were young."

Her huge eyes filled to the brims with tears. Jacob swallowed. What the hell did he know about talking to people about anything of substance? He'd already proven it with River. He knew nothing at all. Had he been asleep his whole life? And now that he seemed to have awakened, he worried that all his walls were falling. How many more was he going to let into his heart?

"I'm sure what you and River went through was incredibly difficult." He slipped his gaze to her and took another breath or two before he continued. "My mum died before I could remember her. I always thought I was lucky for that. Death is a rough thing for a kid. Your mother didn't die though. I think what she did is worse."

She spread her gaze over the water. "Yeah, it is. Our mother was selfish. She didn't think of us. I know that." She wiped her eyes and her nose. "Maybe, after all these years, it's just easier to blame the dragon."

HE WANTED TO comfort her but he wasn't sure what might come from his mouth next, so he pulled his hand from his pocket and put it around her shoulder. She didn't move away when he dragged her closer and walked with her toward the path from Urgha.

"Is it after River? After us?"

"No," he promised, praying he was right. He released her and took a step closer to her sister. "You don't have anything to worry about. I'll protect you."

"Okay. Can I tell Graham?"

"I'd rather you didn't, but I suspect you will." He couldn't help but smile when she grinned. "And get rid of the pictures you took of me please."

"I will," she promised. Then, "You were pretty awesome back there. Never thought I'd see a dragon…or four of them. How many are there?"

"Just four."

She cut him an incredulous look. "*Just* four—and you're all in Harris?"

Jacob blinked at her and then turned slowly to Garion. *He has us all here together.*

He had us in Fiji if that was his plan, his brother-in-law said catching up.

No, Jacob thought to himself, sick to his stomach. An element had been missing before.

He couldn't find us in Fiji. None of us had turned. Is it a coincidence that I came to Harris as Drakkon, had an encounter with River, then a few weeks later Red shows up here and kills her cattle?

You think he can track Drakkon? His sister joined the conversation.

Jacob hoped not. If the Red had figured out a way to track Drakkon then he was here because of Jacob.

"How many Onyxes are there, Garion?" he asked out loud, including River and Ivy in the discussion. He hadn't wanted her to hear the first part of the conversation, that this might be a trap meticulously planned out by an enemy Drakkon.

"Only this one."

"Is there any other way to track us?"

His brother-in-law shook his head. "I don't know. I've only lived on the earth with six other Drakkons in my lifetime. I've never had to track any before Red and I used the Onyx to do it. But I can tell you this. Jeremy isn't stupid enough to think he can fight the three of us. That's why he's hiding. His plan, once he found you, was to fish me out."

"Still," River pointed out, "that doesn't tell us how the Red found Jacob, when none of you can find him."

Jacob groaned inwardly.

"I seem to remember reading something in one of Father's books about Drakkon," Helena offered, paying no attention to Jacob's groan growing a little louder. "It was something about tracking them by star song. It was in the part he wrote about Marrkiya and how they had tracked him and used the Phoenix Amber to transform him while he flew."

"What are you talking about?" Jacob asked, but he suspected with a sinking heart, that he knew.

"Of course, this was never proven," she went on, "but Father's claim was that the stars sing for Drakkon...which we all know now is true. Unlike the life mate song, which anyone who has ever lived as Drakkon can hear, the music of flying is more subtle and can only be heard by the most astute ear."

The music of flying. Then it was his fault Red was here. His fault her cattle were killed. His fault she was almost eaten today. He lowered his gaze to his feet.

"Jacob?" River asked, going to him and resting her hand on his arm. "Do you think the Red followed you here?"

She hadn't read his thoughts. She didn't need to.

"Yes," he answered, glancing up at her, not knowing what to expect. Not expecting compassion...the warmth of tender affection.

"I don't care," she told him softly, quietly. "I'm glad you came."

CHAPTER FIFTEEN

JACOB SAT AROUND the table in a kitchen too small to house bodies such as his and Garion's together. The table was cramped and he and his brother-in-law sat at the outskirts, but they made it work and conversation and laughter flowed easily.

They'd all worked together to whip up a meal of sirloin steak sautéed in mushrooms, roasted tomato, and peppercorn sauce, with seafood linguine to go with it. Jacob knew it was going to be a good night while he'd steamed the prawns and made the linguine sauce under River's direction. It had all been a little chaotic, but comforting to Jacob in an odd, warm sort of way. He'd especially enjoyed it when River kicked Garion and Carina out of the cooking area. His brother-in-law hadn't been happy about it, taking offense on Carina's behalf, but River hadn't backed down. In the end, Garion had left the kitchen and took his cat with him.

They'd made amends at dinner, when River prepared a dish of food for the feline, proving the fastest way to Garion the Gold's heart was through his cat—and his wife.

River had it all under control, winning hearts with gracious smiles and sharing whispers and bursts of laughter huddled close to Helena.

Jacob didn't mind that he might be the one they found so amusing. He was glad they were getting along. He didn't interrupt or eavesdrop, but simply took in the sounds and sights of the people he cared about around the table. He belonged to them and they to him.

"River," he said from across the table, bringing her gaze to him. He'd never killed anyone before, but he would. For her. "Did you tell Helena about your music?"

"Your music?" his sister stopped eating and asked.

River's cheeks went as red as the thick braid falling over her shoulder. She tossed Jacob a nervous glance. "It's just stuff I write down."

"River's music is really good," Ivy defended, smiling at her sister. "She just sold a piece to my boyfriend's band."

Interest piqued, Helena put down her fork. "I'd like to hear something."

Be careful, Jacob said inside his sister's thoughts. *Her music sounds like the stars. It will draw Drakkon.*

Helena turned her eyes on him. *All Drakkon? Or just you?*

He knew what she was implying—on both counts. Had it been River's music that drew the Red? Or was his heart the only one so affected? *I don't know.*

Garion and I need to hear it.

"Of course," River allowed, answering Helena's spoken request. "After dinner. But I must confess, Jacob told me you play for the Philharmonic. If you hate my work, I'll be crushed."

"She won't hate it," Jacob assured River gently, winking at her.

What's going on with you and this girl, Jake? His sister's voice broke through his thoughts and the conversations going on around him.

"What do you do for a living, Mr. Gold?" he heard River's father ask.

"I'm in investments and, please, call me Garion."

Your eyes light up like stars when you look at her, Helena interrupted.

Was it that obvious to River? Jacob curled his mouth at her while she brought her glass to her lips.

*She's...*he began and then stopped to begin again. *She makes me feel.*

Feel what?

Everything.

Helena knew him better than anyone else. But she didn't know everything. She was the only family—the only constant—he had in his life. He wanted to tell her what was happening to him, ask her what he should do about it.

Something's waking up in me, coming to life...I don't know, but I can't harness control over it. It's not Drakkon, Helena. It's more wild than that. It's stronger than all my willpower. There are moments when I...I would give up anything to be with her.

Oh, his sister's soft voice sounded in his head. Her expression from where she sat beside River was stunned and she was a bit overcome. *Wow.*

Yeah, I know. I resisted but—

It's difficult, she agreed. *I know. Jake,* the sound of her voice changed, weighted with regret when he heard her again. *We will...ehm...we'll talk about it later. But there's something you should know now. She's not a descendant. I checked the Elder Scrolls on my phone after seeing her eyes. She has eyes like an Aqua. There were no Wrays on it.*

Her mother's name?

It doesn't matter. Wray would be included in the line.

I'll find out what it is, Jacob insisted. *We'll check next time we get WiFi.*

Garion has a mobile hotspot. But Jake, Garion won't turn her even if she is a descendant. He won't even turn his sister. He wouldn't turn Red. That's why we're here.

He turned us, Jacob reminded her.

We were dying.

Jacob turned his gaze on River. *So is she.*

I get it. I really do, but Wray isn't on the list, Jake. It may not be up to Garion. Your time with her will be too short.

No time. The finality of it was something he had to face. But not now. *Maybe I'll take what I can get.*

Later, they carried their tea into the sitting room while the women made the sleeping arrangements.

"I'll lay out fresh sheets on my bed for you and Garion—"

"We wouldn't dream of putting you out," Helena declined. "We'll sleep on the sofa."

"Nonsense," River argued. "The both of you will never fit on the sofa. I'll sleep with Ivy and Jacob can sleep out here."

They talked about dragons, without giving up too much to River's father. They didn't tell him about Charlie Owens because it would lead to too much explaining. Garion also didn't tell him that he and his wife were Drakkon, or that Marrkiya the Aqua, or Marcus Aquara, as he was now known, was his foster father. But when Mr. Wray excused himself for the night and Ivy ran off to see Graham, to whom she'd probably spill her guts, Jacob told River about the Aqua.

"Is this all a gigantic coincidence?" she asked him from her chair, asked the three of them. "How are we all tied together like this?"

"I don't believe in coincidences," Garion told her. "This is in the stars."

Her gaze settled on Jacob. She smiled softly and then grew serious again. "What does the Red have to do with my stars?"

"Nothing," Garion told her. "He's not here for you. He's here for me, for my blood."

The Red sounded like a horrible creature. "Tell me about him," River asked, settling into her chair. "Jacob told me he was once your friend."

"His name is Jeremy Redmond," Helena began, moving closer to Garion on the sofa. "He was Garion's best friend. He knew what Garion's blood could do and he wanted to be altered. He wanted Garion to fill the sky with Drakkon. He still does."

"I refused," Garion picked up. "He shot Helena. She was in my arms at the time—"

"—about to tell him that I loved him."

"The bullet went through her and into me," Garion continued.

River covered her mouth with her hands and then shook her head in amazement. "And you both lived?"

"Garion healed me," Helena said, "altering me in the process."

River's eyes widened like moonlit seas on Garion as their words sank in. "You can heal people?"

"Only if they're descendants of true Drakkon and I alter them. But I don't want to fill the sky with Drakkon. I don't plan on ever doing it again."

"By the way," Helena interrupted with a smile aimed at River. "What's your mother's maiden name, River?"

"Rodin. Why?" River narrowed her eyes and then smiled. "Do you think I might be a descendant?"

"I did," Helena answered candidly. "But Wray is not on the scrolls and normally it would be cross-referenced."

"That's a little disappointing," River confessed with a slight sigh. "I'd like to help you stop the Red. He did almost eat me." She turned her attention back to Garion when he shook his head.

"Why did you alter Jeremy?" she asked him.

"I didn't. I altered into my Drakkon form and bit off his arm that was holding the gun he was shooting at me. After I left, he mixed his blood with the blood I left behind."

She listened and nodded and then looked at Jacob. "Why did you alter Jacob?"

"Red had come to my home in Norway. He flew through the window of my villa and pierced Jacob with his talons."

"Pierced him with his talons?" she asked, bringing her hands to her chest and staring at Jacob as if his death would have been the worst thing imaginable. "You didn't tell me that about him."

Jacob did everything he could not to leap to his feet and go take her in his arms. "I didn't want you to be more afraid of what Drakkons can do."

"Jake would have died if I hadn't changed him."

River barely looked at Garion when he spoke. "I'm glad you did."

Jacob wanted to agree, but he was no longer sure he did. He loved flying, being Drakkon. He thought it was all he'd ever wanted. But River made him want to be a man. He didn't know what to say, so he smiled instead and bit his tongue when his sister asked if she could read her music.

Jacob remained silent while River hurried to her room. How could it be that he would give up everything he'd ever wanted for her? Was this love? Could she be his life mate? If she were, he would never get over her death. Drakkon only had one life mate.

Maybe he was worrying over nothing. The stars sang for Drakkons, not humans. Helena had heard her life mate song when she was human, but she was a descendant, soon to be a Drakkon. River was not.

Garion, can a human with no essence be a Drakkon's life mate?

Yes. My mother possessed no Drakkon essence when she and Marcus heard the music. It's the reason he asked the Elders to use the Phoenix Amber to take the last of his essence so that he could live out his life with her and die with her.

Jacob didn't know. They'd never spoken about Garion's family. Jacob had spent hardly any time with the newlyweds on the island. When he spoke to Garion, it had always been about training the Drakkon.

So, it was possible that River could be his life mate. That he could love her and grieve over her forever. Wonderful.

The Phoenix Amber will not work on you, Jake. I tried as a child and it didn't work. You have my blood.

Jacob slid his gaze to him. *I didn't—have you been in my head, Garion?*

No, he's been in mine. Helena sent and wiped her eye. *You love her.* She sounded as stunned and unsure how to feel about it as he did. She knew River was the first woman he ever opened his heart to. She knew what his immortality meant. It brought tears to her eyes where Jacob had never seen them before.

River's return pulled their attention to her. Jacob was glad for the distraction she provided, but he should run.

"I brought something I wrote a few months ago." She handed her sheets and new guitar to him. "You've already heard it."

The music she'd hummed to him. The music that scattered his willpower to the wind and beckoned him to fly. "I'm not sure I—"

"Oh, can't you?" she asked, frowning. "I was hoping I could hear you play it."

He took the guitar and smiled, though his sister's voice came through asking him if he was okay. No, no he wasn't. What if he started playing and busted out of his clothes? He'd bring the ceiling down, not to mention what it would do to River's poor father seeing a Drakkon in his sitting room.

River left him with the music and the instrument to play it and sat down in the chair close by to listen and watch. Was he really going to take the chance of not only hearing her music, but playing it? His will wasn't that strong.

He blew out a heavy breath and read the music first. He could hear it in his head. He remembered the sound of her humming it to him. He began to play. His fingers had mastered the strings years ago. He'd played thousands of songs—his and other's. This melody went beyond anything he'd heard before. It was textured with emotion, both dark and light, a mix of harmonic and staccato notes that restored and stimulated him.

He fought to steady his breath, to control the desire to take to the sky. It was too difficult. Looking at her while her sound saturated every fiber of him nearly made his fingers pause twice. He felt Drakkon rise up within as tears streamed down River's face at the sound he produced. He understood its effect and why it was so profound. It was his heart through her eyes. His Drakkon heart.

He wanted to respond. He wanted to snatch her away from the world, guard her as his treasure, and take her to places she'd never been before, to heights only he could take her.

He felt the fire expand within, heating his gaze, tightening his muscles.

Garion stood up before he did, a warning glinting in his gold eyes. *Control it, Jake.*

Jacob rose and set down the guitar. He took a second to exhale then looked at his sister.

"It was remarkable. One of the most beautiful pieces I've heard in years," she said, a bit breathless. *But as far as drawing Drakkon,* she continued in his head, *it would seem to be only you, Brother.*

"I may know some people interested in your kind of sound," she told River out loud.

But that doesn't mean she's your life mate, Garion's voice returned. *It will be the stars' song that sings to you, not hers.*

But hers meant something, Jacob told himself. It made him want to be Drakkon. In the last forty-eight hours, it was the only thing that did.

He didn't want to control it, not after today. Another Drakkon had tried to take her from him today. Jacob's wrath went unsatisfied. Tonight, he wanted to rule the sky.

"Excuse me," he murmured and moved past them to the door.

The moment his feet touched the dirt, he took off running. He leaped over rocky declines and swerved sharply to avoid nesting gulls that didn't see him coming.

Jacob? Her voice going through him pulled him back. *Where are you?*

The part of his heart that was man wanted to rush back to her, take her in his arms, kiss her, make love to her. How could he let this happen to him? If he stopped wanting to be Drakkon, he'd never fly again. Was he willing to truly give it up for her?

Why did you leave?

Drakkon faded and Jacob's heart broke a little at its submission.

Because, he told her, *this is what I've always wanted.*

CHAPTER SIXTEEN

RIVER KEPT HER eyes toward the sky as she made her way to the cliffs. She didn't know why she was searching for him. He was doing what he'd always wanted. That wasn't what bothered her. She'd never told him not to, but he said it as if she had. He was the one who had tried to charm her. She'd never asked him for any promise of devotion. Go be a dragon. Have fun!

It was his sister and brother-in-law who'd expressed concern over him turning, not her. They worried the dragon hunters would discover him. River figured if they hadn't found the Red, they wouldn't find Jacob.

She would though. She'd stay here all night until he returned. She wanted to tell him she didn't care about him flying…about him. But she'd be lying about one of those things. She was a fool. This was her fault. She knew he'd leave. They always left.

"I didn't leave, River."

She startled at the feel of him behind her, sinking his face into her hair. He inhaled her, slowly, deeply, drawing her in as if her scent made him whole and there was much to put back together. She couldn't think enough to stop herself from shaking. She angled her face, drawn by his breath along the column of her throat but she lost him in her line of vision as he drifted back behind her with the subtlest nuance of movement, catching her breath, making her body quake. He swept his nose down the other side of her throat with the barest trace of his lips in pursuit.

She felt lightheaded with desire. Her blood burned in her veins. The heat was almost painful. She wanted release.

He swayed around to stand in front of her, keeping his face close to her skin, his eyes aflame on hers. He took her face in his hands and tilted her head slightly upward, moving over her, driving her mad with the closeness of his mouth. "You are my desire," he whispered, leaning in and closing his eyes. "You're what I've always wanted."

River was sure he could feel her heart slamming against him. Her bones disintegrated when his lips brushed the corner of her mouth. He caught her in the crook of his arm and pressed her against him.

Molten flames engulfed her as he spread his tongue over the pulse at her throat. His deep groan echoed through her and shook her in his arms. He kissed his way back to her mouth and covered it, devouring her. She closed her arms around his neck for support but it only made him feel harder, tighter. His lips molded and teased her. His tongue stroked the deepest corners of her aching mouth in a masterful dance of seduction that set fire to her blood.

He stopped kissing her suddenly and looked into her eyes. "Do you hear that?"

She listened, too eager for more of him to hear anything at first. And then, like bells sounding in the distance, a melody took form in her head and made her want to fly.

"Music," she whispered close to his mouth, afraid that if she spoke any louder, the music would fade.

His smile washed over her like sunshine after a hurricane. "Music from the stars, River. You're my life mate."

"Oh," she breathed. "I am? Is it like someone you're supposed to marry?"

He grew serious suddenly and turned a little pale. "Married or not, life mates will always be drawn to each other, belong with each other and no one else—forever."

He said the last word so low that River almost didn't hear him.

"You're afraid of having that with me," she said in an equally quiet voice.

He traced her lower lip with the pad of his thumb. "No, I'm not."

He moved closer, his breath still as he pressed his face to her cheek then dipped his mouth to her neck. She leaned her head back, offering him all.

He withdrew slightly. "River, do you trust me?"

"Yes," she said without hesitation.

His smile singed her nerve endings. She watched him step back and pull off his shirt. Her eyes drank him in. She ached to go to him and run her teeth over his chiseled torso, the long, lean muscles in his arms.

Her gaze fell to his abdomen where his fingers worked his jeans loose. He was taking everything off to alter. Her mouth went dry. Her hands, her bones, shook as he pulled his shapely legs free of his jeans. He stood before her in his snug boxer briefs, glorious to her starving eyes.

"Remember, trust me." He smiled and backed away. "I won't hurt you."

She nodded, marveling at what was about to happen. When nothing did, she quirked her brow at him.

Sing to me, he suggested, closing his eyes.

She began to hum the song he'd played on the guitar. She watched his eyes open on her, blazing blue-gold furnaces. Drakkon's eyes. She understood now why he'd left the house in such a hurry. Her music made him turn. She kept humming in his head. She swore she saw the moonlight glint off the beginnings of a fang when he curled his mouth at her. He changed so quickly that, for an instant, he became a giant blur. But when the dirt settled, her vision was clear enough.

She would never get used to the size of him, the power in every nuance of movement, the radiance of a star come to life. He snatched the breath from her lungs, exposed all her vulnerabilities, and made her want to weep at the privilege of winning the heart of a Drakkon.

Still, when he dipped his mighty head to her, she fought not to run away. Who wouldn't be afraid standing at the tip of a dragon's snout? He breathed in her scent and she reached out her hand, trusting him not to bite off her fingers.

Climb up my neck, River.

What? No—

Your family's safe with Garion and Helena. Come away with me for a few hours. We won't go far. I promise.

Come away with him? How many human beings would ever receive such an invitation? She wasn't going to let this chance to do something magical and terrifying slip away. She turned back to get his clothes.

Leave them.

A thread of heat slipped down her spine and made her face go warm. He was taking her away from here. When he landed, he wasn't going to need his clothes.

She left them and lifted her foot to his neck. His scales clinked like ivory on metal, giving her pause to press her weight.

I barely feel you. Keep going, he urged.

She made her way cautiously up his neck then down to the small niche between his shoulders. She stepped on his spikes for leverage and gripped others for support. Every part of him was too big to straddle. She had to rest with her legs stretched out behind her.

Was this really happening? She thought to herself as she looked out over Maraig and the loch from high above.

Jacob, there's only your spikes to hold on to. I'll fall.

I'll catch you.

Her belly flipped and they hadn't even taken flight.

He flapped his great wings and his body lifted off the ground. River squealed and pressed her body close to his. She closed her eyes but opened them again. She didn't want to miss the spectacular view.

He rose on a slight incline, keeping her steady and balanced. The wind snatched her breath, but she hunkered into the small nook of muscle and bone and found herself protected from the worst of the wind by his scales. The power in his wings swinging high then low, bringing them higher and farther set her heart to racing. She was riding a dragon, falling madly in love with the man whose heart the dragon possessed.

The man and I are one, River, she heard the smoky cadence of his voice in her head. *When you speak to Jacob, you are speaking to me. When I kiss you, touch you, I—oh, shit...*

River lifted her head. What did he just say? His body rumbled and tightened beneath her. Something was happening. He was fighting something. She could feel it.

Jacob, what is it?

Don't be...afraid.

His scales grew soft beneath her fingers. Oh, shit was right. He was turning into a man! In the air!

He moved as fast as the wind tearing at their hair as they plummeted toward the mountain range below. He swung her around in his arms and held her close. *I've got you*, he whispered in her head. *I took skydiving. I know what to do.*

She wanted to laugh at the ridiculous idea of Drakkon skydiving. She also wanted to cry at how safe and adored she felt on the way to her death. At how insane she'd actually become. She didn't have time. He pulled back, and with a smile that heated her blood—even now, he became Drakkon once again.

He snatched her from the air with his talons and rose sharply toward the clouds, holding her close to his heart. She could feel its mighty thumps against her, hear them in her ears when she pressed her cheek to his chest.

I'm sorry, River.

Why did that happen?

You make me want to be a man.

But hadn't he told her that he'd always longed to fly? That his dreams had come true? Was she keeping him from them?

And that's all it takes? she asked. She closed her eyes to keep them from leaking. She didn't know how to stop making him want to be a man because she wanted him to be one, too.

That's all it takes.

Should I sing then?

For now.

He flew them to the Isle of Skye, past Portree to a remote bay called Camasunary. He landed at the edge of the sandy alcove and set her down.

The moon hung low in the sky, casting dancing light over the water and covering the snow-tipped mountains in a pearly glow.

But it was the sight of Jacob's naked body in the moonlight that made her heart skip. His sculpted physique and long, shapely legs made her want to stare at him for eternity. His long, heavy cock dangling between his thighs made her want to do a host of other, more primal things to him.

He came close, stopping when he had to tilt his head to look at her.

She lifted her hand and stroked a strand of his silky hair falling over his shoulder. There were many things she wanted to ask him about life mates, and flying, and their future. But it could all wait. There was Drakkon fire in his eyes, desire that burned through her flesh and bones and turned her heart to cinders.

Would he be able to control it? Hadn't he said just this morning that he didn't know how dangerous he was or the extent of his desire? Too late to worry about it now. She'd known what she was doing when she climbed on his back.

"I don't use protection," she told him. "There was no need."

He turned his face into her hand and kissed her palm, never taking his eyes off hers. "I took care of it permanently in Fiji. We can't have little Drakkons running around."

He leaned in and kissed her jaw, moving lower to her neck. He was hungry, but so far patient and restrained—and more irresistible because of it.

He slipped his warm hands under her sweater and lifted it, running his fingers up her sides as he undressed her. He withdrew from kissing her throat and pulled the sweater over her head, watching her hair spill around her shoulders.

"Do you know how beautiful you are to me, River?" he asked softly, finding her gaze in the moonlight.

She nodded. He made her feel beautiful every time he set his eyes on her.

He coiled his arm around her back and hauled her against him. With one fluid movement, he hefted her up over his hips. He captured her breath with his mouth and coiled her legs around him. He carried her closer to the water's edge and dropped to his knees in the sand.

She was really going to do this. She had no doubts that it was right with him. She'd never wanted anything as much as this. She wanted him with every part of her body and soul.

His mouth curled into a ruthlessly sexy grin. *I heard that.*

He cupped her neck in his palm and kissed her mouth, breathing with her, tasting her. When she groaned, wanton and wild for him, he teased her with a flick of his tongue over her lips. He bit her chin and raked his teeth down her throat to her breasts. His hair swept over her like whispers. Her nipples pushed against the satiny fabric of her bra, eager to be in his hands, his mouth.

He took them in both, rolling them in his fingers, biting them with his teeth. He made a sound like a starving animal and proved that his patience and restraint had run out when he tore her bra away with his hands.

She lay exposed to the fiery depths of his gaze, burning her wherever it fell. He scooped her breasts in his hands and dipped his mouth to each, sucking her, growing more wild for her. He kissed his way down to her belly and flicked open her jeans. He rose up between her knees to pull them off her, dragging her panties away, as well. He stared at her spread before him and kissed the inside of her knee.

River still wasn't sure this was all really happening. Was this beautiful, magical man about to make love to her? He was ready for her. His cock was big and hard and jutting upward.

He moved over her on all fours, dipping his nose and his lips over every inch of her. She quivered, wanting him to devour her. When he reached her mouth, he paused to look into her eyes and whispered, "I wonder what the stars will do."

She felt a warm droplet fall from him onto her. Her body clenched, aching for more. She spread herself wider, inviting him in. "Let's find out."

"Yeah," he agreed in his sinfully sensual voice, and a smile to go with it.

He kissed her and dragged his mouth over her tight nipples while he sank halfway into her. He paused when she cried out and returned to gaze deep into her eyes. *Do you want me to stop?*

She shook her head and clamped her thighs around him. His eyes darkened and, for a moment, all mercy fled the fire. He lifted his hips, bringing hers with him, and cupped her ass in one of his hands. He coiled her hair around his other hand and tugged back her head, exposing her throat to his hungry mouth. He ran his tongue over her like a flame and buried himself deep inside her.

She grasped his shoulders but he continued to move, undulating slowly, moving to music as ancient as time itself. He swayed against her like the waves rolling in a few feet away.

He let go of her hair and traced her parted lips with his fingers. "River," he whispered and kissed where he'd just touched. "You're the first woman I've ever loved and you will be the last."

His words were like music blending with the stars' song. She loved him and trusted him completely.

"You are the first man I've ever loved," she told him, "and you, too, will be the last."

He covered her mouth with his and thrust his body inside her. Holding her, he pulled her over on top of him. When she straddled him, he drew himself up, his belly tense and tight. He cupped her rump in his hands and moved her over the full length of him—and there was a lot of him, up and down, harder, faster, until the friction between their bodies became explosive.

River tossed back her head, lost in ecstasy—in the feel of him, the sight of him watching her with fiery eyes. She had never felt like this before with anyone else. Waves of pleasure cascaded over her, arching her back, parting her lips, crying out his name while she came on him.

When she fell against him, he lifted her off and leaped away. One moment he was running, and the next, he was flying.

CHAPTER SEVENTEEN

J ACOB REALIZED WHILE he flew that this was a new test of his will he was going to have to control. He couldn't succumb to his Drakkon whenever he had to come. But this was the first time it happened, so he trusted his instincts and got away from her before things got *really* big.

He didn't want to go far. He just needed to cool off before he started burning things. He felt like a living flame, a combustible force that needed release. He somersaulted, confident in his wings, his tail, and his practice. He came back up facing the water and flew toward it. His watchful eyes found River sitting up in the sand, watching him.

Pinning his wings close, he dove into the waves. Almost instantly, his blood regulated to the cold.

Jacob, come back to me.

He burst from the surface, filling the air with water. He soared toward the stars, letting the wind dry him and then returned to the ground...to her.

He approached her slowly on taloned feet. He could smell her. He could smell himself on her.

Do you know how beautiful you are to me, Jacob?

He was glad she wasn't afraid of him. Should she be? Could he control Drakkon around her? He moved closer and swiped her up in his claws. He heard the acceleration of her heart, but she didn't panic. She rested, instead, against his leathery palm and stared up at him.

He lifted her to his snout and took his time breathing her in, letting her scent course through him and awaken his every desire. He remembered the taste of her on his human tongue. He was tempted to taste her now.

Do you want to fly, River?

She smiled, firing up his insides. *Yes.*

Flapping his wings, he lifted them toward the heavens. He went as high as he could take her without her feeling ill. He clutched her to him and inclined his head to her.

I've never felt contentment, he told her. *Even after flying, I feared I still hadn't found what filled the emptiness.*

His scales changed to flesh. His wings receded, and he fell with her in his arms.

I don't feel empty now.

He pulled her closer while their hair snapped above them and kissed her mouth. He'd gone up high, so they had several seconds, at least. He used the time to work his tongue over her throat and wrap her thighs around him. She wasn't afraid. He could never do this with her if she didn't trust him. Her courage was the sweetest perfume, a sexual lure he couldn't resist.

He impaled her with a deep thrust as they fell, once, and then again, grinding his teeth. He withdrew and altered before they struck the water. He carried her back up and let them fall again, entangled in each other's arms, connected by their flesh, their thoughts, and their hearts. He soared toward the music playing for them, twirling and dancing with her held tenderly in his hand, nestled near his heart.

He'd never felt love. Not like this. He thought he never would. He hadn't wanted to, especially not with a mortal. But he loved River. He would do anything for her, give anything for her. But maybe, he didn't have to give up flying after all. She liked it.

She liked being taken in the air. She remained wet and ready for him despite him having to alter every few minutes. It drove him mad.

On the way down for the last time, he moved with her in a primal dance of decadence and desire until he erupted inside her, filling her to overflowing.

Later, he sat with her against the rocks beyond the water's edge. She rested between his legs, cradled in his arms, her head on his chest. He never wanted to let her go.

She was his life mate. The only woman he would ever love until he was no more. How would he live without her? How would he tell her that he was immortal? She possessed no Drakkon essence. Why would she care what the stars said? What if she wanted no part of growing old alone without even a child to prove what they had was real? How twisted and unfortunate was it that he should finally find what his heart had been searching for, only to lose it again and be cast into eternity with nothing, no children, no family of his own making. He felt something in the pit of his belly grow cold.

None of it mattered now. He was here with her, about to share his life with her. If his time with her was limited, he would treasure every moment.

She told him of her mother, with a very different view of her than Ivy had. Jacob remained silent, listening. Lena Wray had been twenty-nine, six years younger than her husband when she ran off with Brant Olson. She was a dreamer, like her eldest by a little over a minute daughter.

"I used to love watching her do the simplest task," River's satiny voice drifted to his ears. "Her hair would fall over her smile and catch every color of the sun."

"Like yours," he remarked quietly.

"What? No," she laughed. "Hers was more vibrant—like her spirit. She made scrubbing dishes fun. I adored her. I used to lay in bed at night afraid of her dying. I never thought she'd leave us by choice."

He didn't need to touch her thoughts to know that what her mother had done made it hard for River to trust. It made her trust in him all the more priceless.

"I won't leave, River," he promised.

She lifted her head and tossed him a playful smile. "You're my life mate. You have no choice."

"It wasn't the stars that made me fall in love with you," he told her, lifting his fingers to her cheek.

"What was it then?"

Jacob, Garion's voice in his head interrupted. *We have a bit of a problem.*

Garion? Jacob sat up. "It's Garion," he told River. She sat up as well. *What's wrong?*

There's a group of people gathering in front of the house with flashlights and lanterns. They're calling for the "dragons". You need to bring River back before the sun rises so they don't see you flying. Try to figure out a way to convince them that what they saw in Tarbert today wasn't real. For now, Helena and I are staying inside and keeping Ivy and her father here, too. I don't want to go out there and have their camera's going off in my face or your sister's. The Bane and what's left of the Elders might not care about finding Red but if they get a whiff of me...

I know. Jacob closed his eyes. *We'll be there soon.*

He told River what was going on and helped her to her feet.

"What are we going to tell them, Jacob?"

"We'll think of something. Come, get dressed." He thought about flying...flying back to Maraig...to help Garion and Helena...nothing was happening. He wasn't changing. He took a step back and raked his hand through his hair. He wanted to be Drakkon. He wanted to fly. He wanted to fly.

"What are you waiting for?" River asked, fastening her jeans and pulling her sweater down.

He looked at her, able to see her in the dim light. What was he willing to give up for her? A sense of grief washed over him for the Drakkon dying in the birth of something new and even more power-ful. He had to *want* to be Drakkon, and he didn't. He didn't want to be immortal. He didn't want to be sterile to keep the world from his offspring.

"It's not happening," he told her, trying not to sound worried. How were they going to get back? Even if they waited until morning, he couldn't take the ferry naked.

She stepped into his arms and ran her hands down the sleek, twitching muscles of his back. She closed her eyes and began to hum. He stepped into her thoughts and saw them flying, and falling, their gasps of ecstasy snatched up by the wind. His powerful wings bringing them higher and higher, clutched to his snowy white chest.

He looked up as the blue hour approached.

He felt himself begin to alter and stepped away from her. He snatched her up in the last moment and hauled her to his back. His wings stretched and snapped, bringing them over the small, empty bothy and the mountains beyond.

It didn't take them long to get back and, thankfully, everyone was facing her house and not the loch. Jacob swooped in below the cliffs, dropped her off where he'd left his clothes and waited until she tossed them over the hill to him.

By the time he altered and dressed, she was already halfway to the house, stomping her bare feet as she went. He followed her.

"What are you all doing here at this hour?" he heard her demand while she parted the small crowd and reached her front door. Not bothering to hide the fact that she hadn't been inside, but on the cliffs with him. She folded her arms across her chest and planted her feet, fearless in the threat of danger. "You all look bent on trouble." She spread her hard gaze over them. "Margery, I'm surprised to see you here."

"And I'm surprised to see you with *him*," Margery countered, scowling at Jacob as he came into view.

"Really?" River tossed her a doubtful smirk.

"Miss Wray." A short, hefty police officer stepped forward and placed his hand on River's arm.

Jacob moved toward them.

Easy, dragon. River's steady voice settled over him. *Let me handle him.*

"Constable Macroy," she greeted in the same tone, out loud.

"How is your father?" the constable asked politely.

"I'm fine," Hagan Wray said, opening the door behind his daughter. "What are you doing here, rousing me from my bed?"

"Charlie Owens was murdered," the constable told him. "I've come to ask River if she knows anything about it."

"And the dragons!" someone from the crowd shouted.

"Dragons?" her father's droopy eyes widened. He stepped out of the doorway and looked out into the small crowd. "Who said that? What dragons?"

Jacob watched him, his breath stalled in his chest. Hagan Wray was about to be vindicated. Jacob wanted this for him. He deserved it. River and Ivy deserved it for the mother who ran out on them.

But they couldn't admit the truth to these people. They were going to have to convince them that what they had seen was some kind of great illusion—that dragons weren't real.

He wasn't sure if he could take away Mr. Wray's long-awaited triumph.

"We saw them!" a man called out. "Two of them! They tried to kill River!"

Her father turned to her, eyes wide, mouth hanging open. "Is this true?"

"No," she told him shaking her head. "Da, I—"

"Jacob didn't try to kill her!" Ivy shouted, pushing her way out the door. "He saved her!"

Shouting erupted over Ivy's confession. People demanded to know who Jacob was. They pushed forward, shoving the constable out of the way. River stood her ground with her family.

"I'm Jacob!" he shouted, drawing every face to his. Silence descended for a moment and he sent his intentions to Garion and then stepped forward.

"He's lying!" a voice shattered the stillness. "He's a man. We want to see the dragon!"

"No you don't," Jacob murmured.

"He *is* a dragon," Margery called out. "I saw him change into one."

"Margery," Hagan called out to her. "You sound insane."

"I have pictures," she insisted with a triumphant grin.

"No you don't," Ivy told her. "You have nothing. None of you do. All you have is your word. Same as my father."

Margery pulled out her phone. Some of the others did as well. Jacob watched their confused expressions. What was going on? What did Ivy know that he didn't? He looked at her, the hint of a smile creeping up her lips.

Ivy. It's Jacob.

He saw her gasp by the door and turn to find him.

Jacob? You're full of surprises.

Yeah. Jacob winked at her. *What's going on with the phones?*

Nothing. It's their pictures. Apparently, when you're a dragon you don't stay photographed. Your image fades. You didn't know?

No. He didn't know.

You were in the pictures I took yesterday while you were flying, she explained. *When I pulled them up to delete them, you had faded from the shot. It's probably why there aren't any clear pictures of dragons around.*

This was good news. Garion wouldn't have known it because he'd kept the Drakkon hidden for so long. But this was good. No one had proof. He could tell them whatever they needed to know to stay safe but they could never prove any of it was real.

Tell Garion. Go, show him. And Ivy...this is big. Thank you.

When she disappeared into the house, he went to stand beside River and her father.

"Everyone, listen," he called out. "You should know the truth."

Jacob, Garion's deep voice warned in his head.

Garion, there's a Drakkon flying around here that's already killed one of their own. They should know what they're up against and they should get the hell away from us. If they aren't aware and Red attacks and kills them, it'll be our fault. They need to know. If you aren't planning to face the Red as Drakkon, then why are you here? If you fight him as Drakkon, people will see. And even if The Bane finds us because of this, we need to do all we can to keep these people safe. Right?

Garion didn't answer right away. Jacob understood why. Everything he'd managed to keep hidden for almost fifteen years was about to be bared in the open. But he was a good guy. He would do the right thing.

Right, he finally said softly.

Jacob turned his thoughts to his sister. *Do you agree? This affects your life as well.*

My life has always been about keeping people safe from Drakkon, she told him. *Nothing has changed.*

Good. Stay inside. No need for them to see who you are.

He turned to River, who shared his thoughts. *And you, my love, do you agree?*

Yes. She smiled at him.

Amidst some demands that Jacob be arrested and the constable arguing with the people around him that he had no grounds yet, Jacob called again for the crowd to settle down.

"I didn't kill Charlie Owens," he told them, "but I know who did. He's bald, about twenty-six, six feet, and he has one arm. He might be wearing Charlie Owens' clothes. If you see him, go the other way."

More shouting ensued. The constable stepped forward and turned to the crowd first. "Everyone step back or I'll take you all in! I won't have chaos or a lynching under my watch. Is that clear?" When they all begrudgingly agreed, he turned to Jacob and River. "You knew who did it and didn't report it to me? I could take you in for obstruction of justice."

Jacob dipped his chin and stared at the constable from beneath his brow. He wouldn't be taken anywhere away from River. He had to convince this man to listen to him and then have him help disperse the crowd. "I didn't report it because there's nothing you can do about it."

The constable stepped back, a look of confusion and fear on his chubby face. He pointed his finger at Jacob's face. "Your eyes changed color."

Jacob was aware of the sound of River's heart thumping, her breath, her thoughts. He pulled back, his point to the constable made. "The man who killed Charlie Owens is like me."

"Like you?" the constable asked.

Jacob nodded as the sun broke over the horizon and bathed him in radiant golden light. "I am Drakkon."

CHAPTER EIGHTEEN

H E WAS EXPOSING who he was to them all. River stepped closer to him. She understood the danger in it. He'd told her about The Bane coming after Garion, coming after him if they discovered that he'd been altered. She was privy to the conversation between him and his brother-in-law. He was doing this to help keep the villagers safe. She loved him even more for it, but she wasn't about to let the crowd hurt him.

"Latham Macaulay," she called out. "You put down that stick before I snatch it from you and beat you over the head with it. Everyone! Listen to me! If you saw the red dragon attack me then you saw Jacob save me."

"Just a minute!" Constable Macroy stopped her, his face pale. "Are you trying to tell me that what these folks allege really happened? That dragons are real?"

River looked at her father and smiled. "Yes, that I what I'm telling you."

"And," Macroy went on, pulling her attention back to him, "your friend here is one of them. So," he shifted his gaze to Jacob, "you can be either a man or a dragon. Is that what you're saying?" He didn't let them answer but laughed and reached for Jacob's arm.

"Constable," Jacob said in a low voice so the others couldn't hear him and stared into his eyes. For a moment, nothing was said between them, but Macroy went white and pulled his hand away as if Jacob's arm were on fire. "I don't want to become that. I want to help. There are two more of us inside. We're the only ones who can take down this renegade. It has already burned and eaten Hagan Wray's cattle."

"It tried to eat you and River," Margery said. "Did it follow you here? You were here in the early spring."

If they thought he'd brought the dragon here, it would get ugly. He preferred to put the blame on them. "It's your cattle that attracts it. It attacked River today because it recognized the scent of her cattle on her clothes." He turned and settled his sapphire eyes on her. "Our sense of smell is very strong."

River looked away to keep from blushing to her scalp. She knew this was no time to think about such things, but she remembered every time she felt his nose or his breath at her neck, her hair—whatever part of her he could breathe in. It was feral and it appealed to her most primal desires. It made her blood go wa…wait. She smelled liked cattle?

"It's had a taste of Maraig," Jacob told the constable, returning his attention to him. "I believe it will come back. You can't kill it with bullets."

"So I'm supposed to trust a man who claims he's a dragon—"

"He is," Margery interrupted, inching closer still to hear what they were saying. "I saw him change into a big, white one."

"How am I supposed to believe this?" Macroy looked up at Jacob and rubbed his creased forehead. "Why shouldn't I just arrest you?"

"Because if you arrest me, you'll be powerless against a dragon."

"Arrest him for what?" River demanded, tired of these threats. "I was with him here yesterday morning. He hasn't left my sight since then. He didn't kill Charlie. As a matter of fact, he hasn't done anything wrong at all. Are you going to arrest him because he told you he's a dragon?"

Macroy looked at the crowd with a defeated sigh.

"I don't want it to hurt anyone," Jacob told him. "I want to stop it. Kill it. That's why I'm here. Constable," Jacob put his hand on the officer's shoulder, "you need to tell these people to go home and stay inside."

We heard the music last night.

What? River blinked at Helena's voice in her head while Jacob continued to convince the constable and the crowd that they needed to leave.

You and Jacob are life mates, his sister clarified. *Garion and I heard the music. The Elders heard it, and Red heard it. It's not like he doesn't already know where we are. Still, it was careless of my brother to do this now.*

But things of the heart can't be controlled, River defended. *Don't be angry with him.*

I'm not angry with him, Helena promised gently. *I'm happy for him that he found you. He's been aimlessly wandering for so long. I'm heartbroken for him because you're not a descendant. You can never be Drakkon, and he can never not be one.*

So? River asked. *Why should that break your heart? I don't care about it and I don't think he does either. Whatever comes, we'll make it work.*

Yes, of course, his sister said. *I'm sorry. I worry about him. Old habits. We should be celebrating, not sitting here waiting for the Red's next move.*

River agreed but she couldn't shake the feeling that there was more Helena wasn't telling her.

Despite her unease, though, she smiled watching the crowd begin to break up, with Constable Macroy directing some to his truck and others to Noah's pickup. It seemed that while she'd been lost in conversation with Helena, Jacob had convinced them to disperse and go home.

"How did you change their minds?" she asked him, moving closer and tucking her hand in his. She didn't mind who saw. In fact, she wanted a few of the girls in the crowd, who hadn't stopped staring at him yet, to know he was spoken for. She wasn't the possessive type, but Jacob was temptation incarnate. With a few well-placed smiles, he'd even convinced Margery to close the shop and wait for him to come tell her things were clear.

"Garion and I had to share some images of the Red with them," he told River, bending his head to her ear. "They're finally convinced of the danger."

"Thank you for telling them the truth," River's father, who was close by, said.

"Doing it may have signed my death warrant," Jacob told him.

"The organization I told you about really does exist. They'll be hunting us soon enough when word of this gets out."

"I'll do my best to help make sure no one talks," her father promised then sized him up from his head to his bare feet. "So, you're a dragon."

"Yes," Jacob nodded. "I couldn't tell you before."

Her father smiled and patted his arm. "I know. You'll stay for dinner? We'll talk more about it then."

River watched her normally unruffled life mate come a little undone at the invitation. He liked this kind of life with family around the table. He'd never had it before. She liked it, too, as long as he was at the table. She no longer felt like she had to run away from her home and her memories. She wanted to make new ones with Jacob.

"Thank you," Jacob finally managed.

"One more thing," her father said, pausing before he turned for the door. "Was Marrkiya the Aqua a man also?"

"Yes," Jacob told him in a gentle voice River loved as much as the rest of him. "He still is. Would you like to meet him when this is all over? His name is Marcus now."

"Would I..." Her father had to stop and begin again several times. Jacob was patient in the waiting. "I never thought...yes," he finally struggled to get out. "I would like to meet him."

When her father left to go back inside the house, River's knees nearly buckled when Jacob turned to give her his full attention. She looked into his eyes where his emotions lay bare. She was growing familiar with what she saw in them. She softened his heart and made it ache. He loved her. He craved her like fire craves oxygen. She loved him. Her head told her it was foolish for letting it happen so quickly, but her heart didn't listen. She already missed lying against the rocks with him, alone with him after a night of flying, and falling, and—

She blushed at the memories they shared. Her heart pounded with reckless abandon when he lifted his fingers to her hair. "I'll show you the world, River," he whispered, having read her thoughts. She wanted to scowl at him but, damn it, how could she?

"I'll go wherever you go, in front of you for protection, by your side, right behind you. I don't care where we live. All that matters about a home is who's in it, not where it is."

"Yes," she agreed, breathless.

He smiled, running his fingers over her lips. "Fiji is nice."

Fiji? Was he teasing? He'd take her to Fiji?

Fiji, he said, touching her mind. *New York, London, Paris, the jungles of Madagascar, I don't care. But right now, I want you to leave. Take Ivy—*

"No!" she said out loud and took a step back. "I'm not leaving you!"

He moved forward in a rush of silky, white-gold hair and hard muscle. He caressed her face in his palms and pulled her closer. "River. Red wants Garion. He doesn't care about you. I want to keep it that way. I want you out of the reach of his jaws. I don't know how long we have and I don't—"

"I'll hide. I'll stay out of the way, do whatever you tell me to do, but I'm not leaving you, Jacob. I'm not leaving."

He closed his eyes and held her close, burying his face in her hair. "You mean everything to me, River. If anything—"

She didn't let him finish but withdrew to look into his eyes. "Nothing will. Now come," she said, taking his hand and leading him into the house. "Ivy will want to go to the Munroes', but I think we're all safest with you, Garion, and Helena."

"River," he stopped her and let go of her hand. "I'm very…"

"What, my love?" She took a step back to him. He didn't answer right away but grinded his jaw. "What is it?"

"I'm conflicted," he finally told her, looking as tortured as he sounded.

"About what?"

"About who I am. Who I want to be. It could make things dangerous if I need to call on Drakkon and I can't."

She remembered what he'd told her. He had to *want* to be Drakkon and she made him want to be a man. As nice as that was to know, she wasn't going to let him give up his dream, just as he wouldn't let her give up hers. "You want to fly."

"I want more than that," he said deeply. "I want you."

She smiled and lifted her fingertips to his face. His voice mesmerized her. Maybe it was the sincerity in his eyes, or his shy, genuine smile that gave her pause to consider how much she loved him. "You have me," she told him. "There's no reason to choose how you have me. You proved that last night and you were magnificent."

She tipped her chin and kissed his jaw. "Magnificent beast," she purred against him. She tossed him a smile filled with wicked intentions, and then left him looking after her like a hungry Drakkon.

JACOB WATCHED THE gentle sway of her hips as she made her way to the door. Only she had the power to heal him. He could be man and beast. He didn't have to choose. Last night was...he thought about it and a smile crept over his lips. It was magic. It defied logic, surpassed the mere physical, and satisfied his every desire. He wanted more nights like it with her. For that, he needed to be Drakkon.

River, he sent to her as she stepped into the house. *Thank you.*

She stopped and turned to smile at him. *Thank me later.*

He would. First he needed to eliminate the threat. After that, he'd take her wherever she wanted go in the world, buy her whatever she wanted, and do whatever he needed to help her become a successful composer. He'd make her days happy until there were no more of them.

And then he'd never fly again.

Inside the house, Garion paced the sitting room with his white cat draped across his shoulders. Helena sat on the sofa with River's father in one of the two chairs.

"I've been trying to contact him," Garion told him while River looked around and then went towards the kitchen. "He won't answer or he isn't listening. He's not in Drakkon form. If he's coming back to try to get my blood, then he hasn't gone far." He shoved the stone into his pocket and scooped Carina off his shoulder. "I'm going to look for him."

Helena leaped to her feet. Jacob held out his arm to stop him when his brother-in-law neared.

"You can't leave, Garion," Jacob told him. "If he gets your blood, everyone is doomed."

"Why does the dragon want your blood?" River's father asked them. "What can it do?"

"Where's Ivy?" River asked as she returned from the kitchen and passed them on her way down the hall to the bedrooms.

"She went to Graham's," her father informed her.

"What?" She stopped and went back to him. "When? Why did you let her go?"

"You know I can't stop her when it comes to Graham Munroe," he insisted. "Besides, it's better if the Munroes don't hear all this talk about Drakkons and Garion's blood"

Garion agreed. "We shouldn't have told everyone. We should have planned something else." He covered his head with his hands then raked his fingers through his hair. "Word will get out."

"When they saw the Red, it was already too late for lies," Jacob said. "Word would have gotten out no matter what we told them."

"About Red," Garion insisted. "Not you. They had no proof!"

"They still don't," Jacob reminded him.

"You told them, Jacob," Garion said, sounding more afraid than angry. "My whole life I'd sworn never to turn anyone I cared about because The Bane killed the first three people I altered."

"I know, Garion," Jacob told him. "Those deaths turned my sympathies toward Drakkon and my heart away from my human family. They changed my heart."

"And mine, as well," Garion agreed, "The hunters are ruthless. They found me after fourteen years and tried to kill me. They tried to kill Helena. They killed Thomas. They made me..." He stopped and closed his eyes. He was weary. Jacob didn't have to read his mind to know it. When he opened his eyes again, his nostrils flared and his jaw clenched. "If either one of you are hurt by The Bane," he vowed in a low, dark voice, "I'll alter every descendant on the list and rain hellfire on—"

"My love," Helena stopped him and stroked his arm. "We'll take care of Red and then disappear."

"We did what we had to do," Jacob reassured him gently. "We don't know where Red is. Now, everyone knows to keep one eye on the sky and one on the lookout for a bald guy with one arm. If it makes them a little bit safer, then we did the right thing."

"I know," Garion confessed with a deep exhalation of breath and a slight smile. "Just protecting my treasure, you know?"

"Yeah." Jacob flicked his gaze to River. "I know. Let's go get Ivy."

She smiled, looking so grateful he was tempted to offer her more. Anything.

Carina, Garion's cat, let out a chilling hiss and darted out of Garion's hands. Jacob remembered being in Garion's penthouse in New York the last time Carina had this reaction. Red was close.

Jacob and Garion were first to the door. It was quiet outside. Too quiet.

Garion ripped the Onyx from his pocket and looked at it, then cursed. "He's here! He's close!"

"Where?" Jacob shouted, searching the sky while Garion began to undress and Helena kicked off her boots. If Red could be seen in the Onyx, that meant he was Drakkon. Jacob's hands shook with the pounding of his heart. He had to keep River and her family safe. Where the hell was her sister?

Ivy? he reached out.

Jacob! She screamed through his head almost bringing him to his knees. *Help me! It's coming!*

He ripped off his shirt and started running.

IVY COULDN'T BREATHE. Her lungs had no more air. Her heart was frozen in terror. She could hear the monster's wings flapping behind her. The red dragon had come! It had come to the Munroes' house and killed Noah with a swipe of its terrible claws. Ivy wanted to scream. She wanted to whirl around and curse the dragon to its face before it ate her. She ran toward the cliffs. She'd rather jump...

Graham.

She came to the edge and looked down at the rocky coastline. The tide was receding. She gathered up her courage and turned to face the monster. She saw Graham. He was running to her. The dragon was flying up behind him. Tears filled Ivy's vision and she almost didn't see the monster take him. She blinked and her love was gone.

Her heart roared as she lifted both of her middle fingers at the beast and then jumped.

CHAPTER NINETEEN

*R*ED! DON'T TOUCH HER! he warned. *If you want blood, don't touch her!* But the Red didn't answer. Jacob's heart was torn to shreds. He opened his mouth and fire issued forth from between his scaly jaws. *Ivy! I'm coming!*

He heard Hagan Wray invoke the name of the Virgin Mary as three Drakkons came to life in his front yard. He took off with Garion flying behind him. *Helena, stay with River, please. Please protect her.*

His sister agreed and made him promise to protect Garion.

Jacob, River's voice broke through the rest. *What the hell is going on? Where are you and Garion going? Is it Ivy? Tell me. Is it? You looked so terrified. Please, this is scaring me. Is it Ivy?*

Jacob couldn't tell her. She'd never stay where she was. He couldn't tell her what he'd heard. She'd go mad by it. He didn't know what to answer, so he didn't say anything. He turned his thoughts to her sister instead.

Ivy? Where are you? Where's Graham? I don't see Drakkon. He waited, searching the sky, searching the earth. *Ivy?*

His resolve faltered. Had the Red found her? Killed her? Kill them both? No, he wouldn't let himself think the worst.

There's a farm. Garion thought to him. *Ivy said Graham lived close by. Helena says he went off the Onyx again. He's walking.*

Jacob's blood rushed through his veins like molten fire. Ivy and Graham were a lure to get them away from the house. *Go back, Garion,* Jacob told him. *He might have come here to get you away from Helena.*

Smoke blew from Garion's nostrils as he sliced his tail across the clouds and turned in the air. *If you find him before I do and he's Drakkon, forget his head. Go for his wings. Take him out of the sky. His head will be easy after that.*

First, I have to find Ivy and Graham. Jacob pulled in his wings and dove toward the farm. *Ivy?* He prayed they were unconscious and not...hell, Ivy couldn't be dead. *Red, where is she? Where's the man? What have you done to them?*

He landed, unaltered and stormed on his great taloned feet toward the house. He picked up Red's scent immediately, but it wasn't fresh. The Drakkon had been here but was gone. Another scent drew him. Human. Not Ivy. He followed it to the pickup truck, parked and still warm just beyond the house. The front door was ajar. Smeared with blood.

Jacob approached slowly, his heart thundering within. Whose blood was it? Graham? He sniffed then cursed inwardly. Noah. River's friend who she loved like a brother. Where was his body?

Fear gripped him the way it had only once before in his life when he was a child hiding behind a tree while a Gold Drakkon burned his house and everyone in it to the ground. *Ivy, where the hell are you?*

He flew over the house and the nearby cliffs listening for any sound of her, smelling the air, hoping to pick up her scent. After ten minutes of nothing, he headed back for the house. What was he going to tell River? The only thing left of her close friend was blood. Her sister was gone. Maybe eaten. The thought sickened him and broke the heart he regretted opening. Love did this—love had changed him, changed his world, and hurt like hell. Ivy and Graham were gone. *Ivy.* He'd promised to protect her, but he hadn't even known she was gone. It was his fault Red was here, his fault Ivy was gone. The weight of it dragged him down.

He felt himself altering and flew low before he tumbled through the air as his wings faded and his talons became fingers. He let himself fall, keeping his eyes open on the sky as memories of Ivy's big, blue eyes filled his thoughts. He descended and hit the water of Loch Seaforth on his back.

He was losing consciousness, sinking into a tomb of cold, murky silence. He heard her voice. "Just don't hurt my sister. Please."

It was just a memory.

I'm sorry, Ivy.

Jacob? It was River. Her voice shattered the shadows and brought the real darkness to light. *Is Ivy with you?*

He'd failed her. He'd failed himself. He'd lost one of his treasures.

Where are you, Jacob? Please, her voice paused on a broken whisper. *Please, come back.*

He opened his eyes and shot toward the surface, breaking free on an explosion of water and pearl-gold wings. It fell to him to tell her the terrible news. As it should. He could delay no longer. He had to pull himself together and be strong for her. He had to protect her and stop Red. Where was the bastard?

Garion, he reached out as the house came into view. He sensed River inside the house with her father and Helena. *Anything on Red?*

No. You didn't find Ivy.

No.

Jacob landed a few feet from his brother-in-law, who was standing by the door and wearing a long, red, hooded fleece robe. He held another one in his hand and tossed it to Jacob when he altered.

"We'll look like a cult."

"It's better than tearing your favorite pair of jeans to shreds," Garion pointed out with a crook of his mouth. "Helena was right about the size."

Jacob felt the insane urge to laugh...or cry. He'd never cried a day in his life. Not once.

But then the front door opened and his eyes filled with liquid as River slipped out into the light.

She took a hesitant step toward him, as if he pulled her with invisible tethers and she didn't want to move.

"Where's Ivy?" she asked on the barest breath. The anguish in her eyes would haunt him forever.

It took every ounce of strength he possessed to speak and not toss off his robe and fly away...away from the pain in his chest, in his belly. Away from the need to take her in his arms and beg her forgiveness. "I couldn't find her."

Somewhere behind Jacob, Garion left. They both knew what not finding her meant.

River stepped closer. Her eyes misted with tears, glistening like twin turbulent seas that threatened to drown him. Her lips parted but, for an instant, nothing but a hollow breath came out. "What...does that mean?"

He would do anything to avoid admitting her worst fear. "It means just that and nothing more. Nothing more."

She reached out her finger and caught the tear coming down his cheek. "Then what is this?" Before he could answer and before she could stop her own tears from falling, she pressed her palm to his chest. "Is she dead, Jacob? Please tell me the truth."

"I don't know. She hasn't spoken to me since..." Since she was screaming for his help. "Since I left. I searched for her, River. I couldn't pick up a scent or a sound—"

"She could be hiding somewhere," she insisted, trying to find hope. "Maybe she got hurt and is unconscious. Did you find Graham?"

"No," he answered softly.

"Maybe they're together!"

He nodded. "Yes, you're probably right."

"I'm going to the Munroes'." She wiped her eyes and turned to start walking. "Noah should be getting back from Tarbert. We need to tell him. He'll help us search for them."

Jacob wished he'd never met her. He regretted staying with her and bringing Drakkon into her life. He clasped her arm to stop her. "River, there was blood. Noah's blood." The sight of her terror-stricken face, her shaking hands reaching for her mouth, was too much for Jacob to bear. He looked away. "I searched for him as well."

"Blood," she echoed, staring at him. "So the Red had been there."

"Yes."

"And..." She paused, waited a moment, and then continued without another tear. "Ivy hasn't communicated with you though you've reached out."

Attention everyone!

Red's voice tore through Jacob's head and set him spinning on his feet, looking around. Helena, having exited the house at some point prior, stood with Garion. Both were armed with pistols and ready to start shooting.

They saw no one on land or in the sky.

Garion reached into the pocket of his robe and produced another gun. He gave it to Jacob without taking his eyes off the hills. "We shoot him if he's still walking. It will give us a minute or two to reach him with our claws. There's a sword by the door, as well."

"How did you get all that through customs?" Jacob asked, not really wanting to know.

"Is it Red?" River pulled on his sleeve.

Jacob nodded and stepped in front of her. *Red!* he demanded, *Where's the girl?*

Which one? Red laughed.

You know which one, Jacob told him scathingly. *The girl from the house west of here.*

"I want to listen!" River pulled on his robe again. "Jacob, let me hear what he's saying!"

No, Jacob shook his head. Not after the question he had just asked Red.

She grabbed fistfuls of the collar of his robe and pulled him down, just enough to level her gaze with his. The strength in her eyes warned him that she would have her way. Her command compelled him to open the connection. "Stop protecting me and let me listen."

Oh right, the girl, Red answered after thinking about it for a second or two. *She was delicious.*

Jacob hadn't let River listen in because he didn't want her hearing anything like this. But he couldn't stop his reaction. Or her from seeing it. Rage and horror drained the color from his skin. Red had eaten Ivy. No. Jacob's eyes fell on River. No, he couldn't have.

River took one look at him and nearly fell apart. She knew he was hearing something terrible about her sister. Her face mirrored his—

horror and anguish vying with fury for dominance. "Let. Me. In," she gave him one last warning.

He did.

...and the older of the two males was sour going down, Red was saying. *He was in love with your life mate. I did you a favor, White.*

Jeremy Redmond.

Jacob wasn't surprised to hear River. He didn't stop her from saying what she wanted to say, and he wouldn't let anyone else stop her. He ached to pull her into his embrace, to offer her his strength. But she didn't need it.

I'm going to kill you, she told Red without any trace of emotion in her tone.

You can't kill me, human. Red chuckled in all their heads.

Garion raised his palm to her, cautioning her against saying too much.

River didn't spare him a glance. She did slip her hardened gaze to Jacob, though, as if something just crossed her mind, adding to her anger. *Yes, I can, Red,* she said slowly, fearlessly, but not foolishly. *And I'm going to do it.*

Jacob looked into her eyes, wanting to promise her his help in killing Red, wanting to promise her anything.

She turned from him and walked backed to the house. He let her go.

You've got yourself a fiery one there, White, Red sneered in their heads. *I might have to take her from you.*

Jacob answered on a low growl. *Come try it, Red. Please.*

I'll see you all soon enough, Red told them and then turned his attention to Garion. *I hope you understand now what I'm capable of. Still, for the sake of our longtime friendship, and because I'm not like the Elders, I won't kill you for what I want.*

You're just as bad as the Elders, Jeremy, Garion corrected him. *You killed innocents, just like they did fourteen years ago.*

You were always soft, Garion, Red drawled. *It makes you easier to control. You forget I know your weaknesses.* He laughed and sounded a little out of breath as if he were swimming or climbing. *I want ten vials of your blood. Refuse and I'll follow you wherever you go and kill people in your life until I get it.*

Garion put his gun in his pocket and untied his robe. "I'm tired of doing nothing. I think he might try to make it to the ferry. He can disappear in Skye and be back here in an hour. I'm going to look for him. Jacob stay here with your life mate and keep her the hell away from Red."

Jacob nodded. River would no doubt try to kill Red herself. He wasn't about to let her get hurt. He wasn't letting her out of his sight.

He backed up when Garion shrugged the robe off his shoulders and became Drakkon. Wide, elongated, yellow eyes swept over his wife. Helena's robe fell to the ground and Jacob looked away as his sister moved out of her flesh and into her scales.

Red, Garion sent out lifting himself high on great, twenty-nine foot wide, gold wings. *You're not getting shit. The more people you kill, the more I'm convinced that Drakkon should never again rule the sky.*

Walking back to the house, Jacob agreed.

CHAPTER TWENTY

R IVER LOOKED IN on her father first. He was napping soundly with Carina, Garion's cat, close by on his pillow. How could it be that Drakkon was once again responsible for a cataclysmic event in their lives? First her mother and now Ivy. Ivy. She wanted to collapse, fall to her knees and bury her face in her hands. They shared birth. How could she be dead? How would she tell her father? What if he blamed her? And why shouldn't he? She'd brought them here.

What did any of it matter anymore? Ivy was gone. Only one thing mattered now—killing the Red.

She blinked back her tears as she shut the door to her father's room. Jacob was waiting for her on the other side. She walked around him and didn't stop on her way toward the kitchen. She didn't want to see him. Not now. She didn't want to be talked out of her decisions. She didn't want to be reminded that he was the same as the thing that had...the thing that had eaten Noah. Had it eaten Ivy, too? And Graham? She thought for certain this would drive her insane for months...years to come.

She hadn't said goodbye. She hadn't even known Ivy had gone. She'd been too busy fawning over Jacob and let her sister slip away.

She pulled in a breath. It was getting more difficult to inhale with each moment. She felt a little lightheaded. She cursed the thought of fainting and stormed into the kitchen. She went directly to the drawer where she kept her knives, opened it, and chose the longest blades.

She heard Jacob enter the kitchen but she didn't acknowledge him while she set six knives on the table. She snatched up a kitchen cloth and tore off six strips.

"What are you doing?" he finally asked her.

"What does it look like I'm doing?" She didn't look up while she kicked off her boots and lifted her foot to the chair to tie the first knife to her denim-clad calf. "I'm getting ready."

He didn't come closer but rested his hip against the counter. "I don't want you to try to fight him, River."

"I don't care what you want." She secured the knife to her calf and went on to her other leg. "The monster killed my sister, my friends. If you think I'm going to sit around here and wait until IT decides to show up, you're wrong!"

The more she had to explain herself, the angrier she became. Though somewhere deep inside she knew Ivy's death wasn't Jacob's fault, she trod upon her logic on feet made of stone and rage. She hated Drakkon for doing this. All Drakkon.

"How do you intend to find him?" he asked in his deep, sensual voice that had become as familiar to her as her own. Disguised slightly as Drakkon, it was the same voice that had first spoken to her in her head. *I don't eat people.*

But there was one that did eat people. She tied two more knives to her thighs and then shoved the last two under the belt around her waist. "I'm going to make a deal with it. One it will be too tempted to refuse. Please don't get in my way." She stepped around the table on her way out.

He moved to stand in her path, blocking the door. His long hair fell around his face, casting shadows in his eyes. "Don't get in your way?"

She tried to move around him. He moved with her.

River.

"No," she said, backing up. "Don't read my thoughts, Jacob. You won't like them."

He flinched as if she'd slapped her. Her eyes stung but she fought back any emotion she felt for him, or for anything else. How could she feel when there was an aching, gaping hole where her heart used to be?

"River, listen to me—"

"Why, Jacob, did you forget to tell me something?" she challenged, folding her hands across her chest. "Like how if the Red is practically immortal, so are you? I was too lost in you to get it until today. Life mates, huh?" She laughed. She'd believed it all. She'd believed they were safe. She'd let him in and believed they were forever. "Until I die and you don't. Helena told me I'm not a descendant. All this life mate stuff sort of loses its significance now."

"Not for me." He looked and sounded as broken as she felt.

She wanted to touch him, to remember laughing with him, flying with him. But Ivy was dead and there was no place for joy or peace in her. "I think it's best if...when this is all over...you—"

"I'm not leaving you."

She couldn't look at him and remain steadfast to her decision. His heavy voice made it difficult enough. "That's not your choice," she told him on a tight breath.

"Yes it is," he said, stepping away. "I know I let you down. I know I brought Red here. There's nothing I can do to make up for it. But I love you and I'm not leaving you."

He couldn't be doing this to her now—tempting her with everything she'd ever wanted since she was eight. But everything was different now. She wanted to go find Red and kill him. She didn't want to go soft and be distracted from her purpose. She didn't want to think about all she'd lost in one day. And she didn't want a Drakkon in her life. They brought nothing but sorrow. "Jacob, this isn't going to work with us after Ivy."

"River," he whispered.

"I don't blame you for her death," she assured him, biting down hard on her teeth to keep herself from falling apart at the sight of his tormented expression. "I blame myself. Please," she begged him on a strangled sob, "don't fight me on this. Just do as I ask."

"I will," he said, moving aside to let her pass. "Just don't ask me to go."

Part of her was glad he didn't give in and leave. He wouldn't leave. It tempted her to wish she was Drakkon so she could stay with Jacob forever. But there was too much sorrow between them now. Her sister was dead…her Ivy was gone because of the three Drakkons she had let into her home. The Red was *their* enemy. Not her family's. Not until now. It wasn't Jacob's fault that Red had tracked him. It was her fault for knowing it and letting her sister out of her sight the morning after the Red had tried to eat her.

She would regret it for the rest of her life. Immortality? No, thank you.

She would let Jacob stay until Red was dead, and then she'd take her savings and leave Harris. She wasn't afraid anymore. She could do it now. She'd changed. Jacob had called her brave. And she was.

She didn't want to think about leaving him, the one true love of her life. She didn't need the stars to tell her he was. But this had become too real. "Fine. Let's go then."

"Where are we going?" he asked, following her out of the house.

"To the banks of the loch. I don't want it swooping in behind the cliffs and surprising us again."

She felt his eyes on her while they walked. She loved walking with him, the feeling of being covered by him, feeling his heat, looking up at the chiseled cut of his jaw. She'd been blinded by him, dazzled by his soft smiles, held captive by the mystery and magic of him.

It had cost Ivy, and Noah, and Graham their lives.

She tried to concentrate on the sounds around her. Twice now, the hum of nature had changed when a Drakkon was near. She didn't need Garion's seeing stone. She had her instincts to rely on.

And right now, her instincts were telling her not to look at Jacob.

"You're making a point to call the Red 'it'."

His voice reverberated with unspoken questions, dreaded anticipation. It seeped through her and into her veins, compelling her to just look up. She didn't.

"That's what it is," she said through tight lips, keeping her eyes on the road. "A thing. A monster."

Silence, imbued with hurt and offense, settled between them, making River regret her words.

"Am I a monster, too?" he finally asked, barely breaking the silence.

His breath along her ear sent a thread of warmth through her. She didn't want to hurt him. She wanted to scream and cry and kill, but she didn't want to hurt Jacob.

She shook her head. "No, you aren't a monster. But it doesn't change anything, Jacob."

Thankfully, he didn't push.

"What deal are you going to offer?" he asked instead.

"The Red wants Garion's blood," she told him. "I'm going to tell him that I have something better."

He laughed but there was no mirth in the sound. "He won't believe it. There's nothing better than Garion's blood."

She finally turned to look at him walking beside her. It was easier when she was thinking about Red. "Sure there is. There's your blood. There's Helena's. And there's the Red's. I'm surprised one of you hasn't already figured it out."

He looked a bit pale. "Figured what out, River?"

"While you and Garion were searching for Ivy, Helena mentioned some things. One of them being that she thinks you and she are becoming Golds. You have his blood now."

"Yeah," he said softly, thoughtfully, and lifted his fingers to his hair.

She should look away, but watching his expressive face as he came to grips with a very possible, very terrible truth, tempted her to never look away again. He understood the magnitude of what this could mean. The Red, with the power in his blood to alter people, would be cataclysmic for the human race.

"You can't tell him," he said on a deep, trembling whisper.

"I don't intend to. But when I make the offer, he must believe that I'm telling the truth."

"If you're right, and he discovers it—"

"He won't," she assured him. "Then you agree he needs to die."

"I never disagreed." He took her arm and stopped to turn to her.

"Do you think I could after what he did? I know what needs to be done, but I don't want you to do it. You're not immortal. Look at me, River! Red can kill you. What do I do then? How do I live after that?"

"The same way I'm supposed to live now," she shouted. "I lost my sister and I…" She stopped. She didn't want to say anything more. Her eyes were burning. Her chest felt like someone had dropped two more boulders on it. She didn't want to cry, to lose control.

"I know."

He didn't know. He couldn't know. But suddenly, it didn't matter. He was here. He hadn't left her since he'd learned of Red. He promised not to leave. Could he stand her guilt, her heavy burden? When they were alone, Helena had told her that Jacob had never been in love with anyone before. In fact, he'd never stayed in a relationship longer than a week or two. River had worried that Jacob wouldn't stay with her either, but his sister reassured her that things were different with him this time and the stars had confirmed it.

And here he was, not running.

"I wasn't there for her," she quieted her voice to a whisper, trying to swallow the terrible sounds that ached to come out of her mouth.

"Neither was I."

Here he was, hurting with her.

She tried to stop the floodgates from opening but he was knocking them down, kicking them aside, ready to catch her in his arms when she fell. She loved him madly, fangs, scales, wings, and all.

JACOB CLOSED HIS arms around her and buried his face in her hair. He didn't think his heart could break any more than it already had, but he was wrong. River's sobs broke through every barrier he'd ever built. He didn't know what to do to help her, so he held her tight and cried with her. After a few minutes, he lifted her and carried her to a rock wall along the bank. He sat down against it and pulled her close.

She tried to speak a few times but her body seemed to exist solely to house her cries.

How had this happened? How had he allowed such harm to come to her? Maybe she was right. Maybe he should leave. She'd be safer without him in her life.

But the scent of her, the sound of her, the feel of her would haunt him. She was everything to him. She was home. She was satisfaction, contentment, the fulfillment of his every desire. He'd never be able to stay away from her.

He'd help her do whatever she needed to do to smile again. But he couldn't let her tell Red anything about their blood.

She was mumbling unintelligible things into his soaking wet neck when he thought he heard something else.

A small, weak voice.

He sat up almost pushing River off him. "A cramp," he explained when she blinked her tear-filled eyes at him.

Hello?

Jacob, it was Red, bringing Jacob to his feet. *After you mentioned my eating a girl—when I hadn't, I went back and had a look around, I found this little morsel with blue hair washed up on the rocks, half-drowned and banged up pretty bad. She probably slipped and—*

Red, is she alive?

Bring me Garion's blood and you can have her. That's all I want, Jacob. You can save her. I don't think it's too late. I could be wrong though.

"Jacob?" River asked cautiously as she rose to go to him. "Is it your leg?"

His eyes poured over her. He could make it all right again. He could get Ivy back without involving her.

"Yes," he groaned.

Red, I have something more valuable than Garion's blood. Tell me where she is and I'll bring it to you. Alone.

"Can you like...open a line so I can speak to Red and make my deal?" River wiped her nose and asked.

Jacob nodded, then pretended to connect them. He listened in while she called to him and felt like hell for what he was doing.

"River," he began. He had to tell her. "I think I—"

What do you want me to think you found, White?

"Why isn't it answering?" River demanded.

Her hair blew across her face like red war paint. A different kind of storm than the one that had just passed brewed in her eyes. Looking at her was like looking at some ancient Pictish warrior queen. She was strong. Stronger than Jacob had given her credit for. She'd let herself grieve and find some comfort in his arms, but now she was back to wanting to fight. He had to keep her away from Red.

"What kind of coward is this son of a—"

"River," he stopped her. He needed to tell her what was going on or risk losing her for good. She would be able to handle it. "It's Red. He's talking to me now. He won't open a connection to you."

Red, he quickly switched his thoughts back to the Drakkon, *like you, I found something. It has tremendous power. I don't want it. I simply want the girl. She has become part of my treasure. We make the trade and Garion doesn't have to know anything.*

"What do you mean he won't talk to me? Why not?"

Jacob looked at her. He'd do anything for her, but he wouldn't let her go.

A part of your treasure, you say? Red asked, his interest piqued. *What can this thing do?*

Everything. It makes the Gold's blood obsolete.

Is it an egg? Red asked with excitement in his tone. *Has a White found an egg yet again?*

We'll talk again soon, Jacob replied and cut the connection, leaving Red wanting more.

"Jacob," she tugged on the sleeve of his robe, "tell him my deal. Tell him to meet me—"

"River," Jacob put his finger over her lips to quiet her. "I think I heard Ivy."

CHAPTER TWENTY-ONE

"RED SAYS HE found her." Jacob smiled looking into River's wide, stunned eyes. "I think she's alive."

"What?" The question came like a high-pitched squeak. "Alive? She's alive?" She swayed on her feet but Jacob held her steady. "Where is she?"

"I don't know yet, but—"

She freed herself from his grip and looked up at the sky. "Where is she!" she roared, her voice echoing off the crags. No reply came, though Jacob didn't expect one.

River turned to him in the stillness, her gaze as hard as granite. "You told him about the deal."

"Yes," he told her the truth.

"Will he meet me?"

"No, River. But he might meet me." He told her what he'd told Red. "He thinks I've found an egg, a magic one, like Garion. He's very interested. Let's give him a little while to let it simmer. But not too long."

"Why?" She pulled back on his hand when he moved to go. "What aren't you telling me?"

Damn it, he didn't want to give her hope and then snatch it away again. He raked his fingers through his hair and set his eyes on hers. "He says she isn't well. She may have fallen from the cliffs."

"What? No!" She yanked her hand away and grasped his wrists. "Jacob, we have to get her back! What do we do? We have to hurry!"

"We have to do this right or we'll lose her," he told her in a calm, steady voice. "He believes I have something priceless that I would give up for Ivy."

"Why would he believe that?" She looked angry enough to punch him. He didn't back away. "It makes no sense. Helena said he heard the life mate music last night. He spoke to me. He knows Ivy isn't the one."

"I told him she was part of my treasure," Jacob explained. "He knows what that means. A Drakkon would give anything to get its treasure back."

Her eyes filled with tears yet again. She bit her lip, drawing his gaze there. "Ivy is part of your treasure?"

"Yes," he told her softly, his eyes going warm and golden. "Your father, too. I'll do whatever I have to do not to lose any one of you."

Her soft smile made his heart accelerate. "I'm sorry for being hard on you before."

He moved in closer, cupping her cheek in his hand. "When were you hard on me?"

Her smile deepened and she turned her face to kiss his fingers. "What do we do? If he can heal her—"

"As far as we know, neither of you are descendants. In that case, even Garion can't help. I'm not giving this information to Red. I'll find her and if she can be healed, I'll do it myself."

"Well, how do we find out if she's a descendant for sure?"

The phones were at the house, along with Garion's mobile hotspot. "I know a way. Come on."

They reached the house a little while later. Jacob was already in contact with his sister.

Where's your phone? I need to see the Elder Scrolls right now.

Why?

I'll explain later, Helena. Please, just tell me what I need to get to the scrolls.

She told him what he wanted to know and remained quiet while he went with River to her room and rummaged through Helena's bag for her phone.

Jacob. It was Garion. *What's going on? Did you find Red?*

No. Where's your hotspot thing?

Jacob. The Gold Drakkon had only spoken his name but the deep rumble was infused with impatience. *We're on the way back and if you don't tell me what's going on, I'm going to kick your ass when I get there.*

One corner of Jacob's mouth hooked into a smile. Garion wouldn't touch him. He was part of his sister's treasure. *Never mind. I found it.*

You don't know the password, his brother-in-law pointed out with a satisfied growl.

Of course, Jacob knew the password. That was the easy part. *Hell, it's your treasures. Listen,* he continued at the change in Garion's breath. *I don't have time for this now. I'll tell you everything when you get here.*

He cut the connection with the couple and sat beside River on her bed. "I don't know when or why the Elders created this scroll, or how the hell my sister found it, but it's a list of every descendant, living or dead."

"But Helena already checked," River reminded him. "She said Wray wasn't on it."

"I know but I want to check your mother's name. It's a longshot." Jacob turned on the device. It asked for a password. He didn't think about it long and began typing.
HELENA/CARINA.
It didn't unlock. He tried again. HELENAANDCARINA

It started searching. He looked up and shared a victorious smile with River.

"So everyone on this list can be altered into Drakkon?" River asked.

"Yes," he answered while he opened Helena's phone and clicked on the app with a skull and crossbones icon.

"Fitting," she murmured.

"Okay, I got it. Hell," he said scrolling down. "There are thousands of names." He typed in the name Rodin. His heart pounded while it searched. The hotspot wasn't strong. Finally...the name Roðinn came up with a link. Jacob swallowed and then remembered to breathe. Was it a variant spelling? What if River's name was on it? It could change his future, his life. She could live with him forever. Garion wouldn't do it. Could Jacob?

"There's something," he managed and glanced up at River. He clicked the name.

Searching...what if Ivy's name was on it? What if they could save her?

"Roðinn – Red," he read out loud when the link finally opened. His mouth went dry. His fingers shook as he scrolled down. "River," he breathed. "I think I found your mother, but—"

"What?" she leaped from the bed and stood to her feet. "But what?"

"Lena Roðinn," he read. "Mated to," he paused and looked up at her. "Stephan Aquatero–Aqua."

"What?" River insisted, drawing her hands to her mouth. "That's not her!"

He read further and closed his eyes. Hagan Wray wasn't the twin's father. He handed the phone to River.

"Offspring," she read on a quivering voice. "River and Ivy Aqua-tero."

It was cause to celebrate. River wasn't just a descendant. Both her parents were descendants. A Red and an Aqua! But neither he nor River smiled.

"My mother—" She choked out and then dropped the phone and ran out of the room.

Jacob followed her. He stopped when her father stepped out of the kitchen and almost walked into her.

"Ah, River. Is there anything to eat?" Hagan Wray asked, completely oblivious to everything going on.

"Da..." She sounded as if she were about to falter, but she straightened her shoulders and pressed onward. "What do you know about Stephan Aquatero?"

His color drained and his eyes widened and then filled with regret. "What...how?" He slid his stricken gaze to Jacob, and then to Garion and Helena when they pushed open the front door and stepped inside. "Aquatero. Was he one of you?"

Jacob shook his head. "Not Drakkon, but a descendant of one."

"Did you know?" River asked him.

"That he's yours and Ivy's biological father? Yes. That his ancestors were dragons? No."

"Wait," Garion stepped forward cloaked in the crimson robe he'd left in the grass. Carina appeared from somewhere and leaped into his arms. "River and Ivy are descendants?"

"From an Aqua and a Red," Jacob told him.

"I knew it!" Helena said and then veiled her eyes from her husband's curious gaze and flaring nostrils.

"I never told you," River's father said, pulling her attention back to him, "because...because Stephan Aquatero was never a father to you. I was. He left before you and your sister were born. Lena came to me and I took her in. I loved you and Ivy as my own. She left because she knew I would keep you both."

River lifted her finger to his weathered face. "I'm sorry you've had such a difficult life Father, filled with so many secrets."

"It wasn't so difficult with you and Ivy in it."

She glanced at Jacob with tear-filled eyes. *What should I tell him?*

They had to do something, Jacob thought to himself. And they had to decide fast. He didn't know how bad Ivy was.

"That's why you wanted the scrolls," Garion accused softly, moving closer to Jacob. "Now you want me to change her."

"Not me," River corrected, hearing him. "My sister."

Garion looked at his wife, who then sent her voice to River. *River, your sister is—*

Alive, Jacob interrupted, hearing their conversation. *I heard her.* He looked at Garion. *Ivy is alive. Red found her smashed up against the rocks. I think she's been unconscious. That's why she wasn't answering me. He says she's hurt pretty bad.*

"Mr. Wray," Garion said politely to River's father, pulling Jacob by the sleeve. "Would you excuse us for a moment?"

They stepped out of the house with River and Helena hot on their heels.

"Even if she is alive," Garion said, turning on Jacob with his cat cradled in the crook of his arm, "and even if somehow we get her back from Red without having to give him my blood, then what, Jacob? I turn her or it's my fault she dies?"

River stepped forward. "You would do the same for your sister, Garion."

Jacob should have known she was descended from the Reds. She was always fearless, always ready to stand and face any obstacle, even if the obstacle was Drakkon.

"I'm sorry, River," Garion said softly and lowered his eyes. "She'll either end up hunting people or they'll end up hunting her."

Jacob scowled at him and then at his sister. Garion wasn't budging. Jacob had expected this reaction. He knew what Garion had given up to keep Drakkon out of the sky. He wouldn't turn Ivy...and he wouldn't turn River.

"So it's better if she's dead?" River demanded, her blue eyes blazing.

"No, of course not—"

"It's you he wants," she cut him off, "but my sister is the one who dies here." She shook her head at him and backed away. "Who are you to make that..." She didn't finish but gasped instead and stared into Garion's eyes. Her own gaze took on a distant, terrified look.

Jacob moved in front of her, pulling Garion's attention to him. His eyes burned like consuming flames behind strands of white gold. "Stop," he warned his brother-in-law.

"I'm showing her a world of Drakkon. She needs to understand what could happen to the world, Jake."

"And you need to understand," Jacob warned on a tight growl, "that this is about her sister, not the world."

He turned his body around and stared into River's eyes, blocking Garion's thoughts from hers. He knew love would be difficult. That's why he'd avoided it his whole life. But it had found him and knocked him dead on his ass. He loved River more than anything else in the world. She was his friend, his lover, his life mate. He wouldn't lose her or her sister to death.

He tugged on the belt of his robe. His hair tumbled back over his bare shoulders as he pulled the robe away. "Hold on to this for me," he said, softly so that only she could hear. He handed her the cloth as his hair and his skin and size shimmered into muscle, and scales, and long sharp claws. He lowered his palm and held it open before River. It hooked him in the heart when she hesitated. He closed his eyes and his hand around her when she finally stepped into it.

He wouldn't lose her to this. To anything. He held her close to his enormous heart and flapped his mighty wings.

Where are you going? his sister asked in his head as he took off.

I don't know. She needs to get away from this and think of a way to tell her father.

Jake.

What.

She was quiet for a moment and then, *Don't do anything that will get you into trouble.*

She'd said it almost every day when he was a teenager, and he'd always given her the same reply. *I won't. Talk to you later.*

He turned his attention to the warm flame pressed gently to his chest. *River?*

Yes, Jacob?

Keep absolutely quiet.

Why? What are we doing?

We're getting Ivy back.

CHAPTER TWENTY-TWO

*R*ED, JACOB REACHED out, *how's the girl?*

The same, Red drawled. *I'm growing bored of all this...and hungry.*

I have the stone.

Stone? Red asked, sounding a little disappointed. *Not an egg?*

What would you do with an egg but be stuck raising whatever hatched from it? No, what I found is jasper. Do you want to know what it can do?

I want to know how you know what it can do, Red replied.

My sister found a way to hack the Elder's files—

The Elders have files?

Yeah, Jacob told him. *Their lore and laws have to be preserved. I asked her to search for jasper in their ancient scripts. She learned that there was this legend of a stone called the Griffin Jasper, like the Phoenix Amber, that could turn any one, not just descendants.*

Interesting, Red took the bait.

There's more, Jacob told him. *According to the legend, the Griffin Jasper gives power over all to the owner. Every Drakkon you alter will do your bidding, and yours alone.*

Red laughed, *And you would give this stone over to me?*

I don't want power. I want the girl.

Then you're a fool, Red scoffed. *But tell me how you know you've found the right stone.*

I used it on my life mate. It works, Jacob assured him. *Now no more questions. Do we have a deal or not?*

All right, White. We have a deal. But how do I know you're not coming here to kill me?

Don't be wherever you are. Leave the girl. I'll leave the stone.

Jacob tipped his head and winked his scaly lid at River. They had a deal. Soon, they would have Ivy back. She smiled at him but was careful not to send him any thoughts.

White, if this is some sort of trick, it's going to get very ugly.

Where are you? Jacob couldn't help but growl. He wanted this to be over so he could begin his life with River.

Cromore in Lewis, Red told him. *There's a small croft house close to the harbor. The girl will be inside. Leave the stone. Hey, hang on…*

Why? Jacob asked. *What is it?*

Nothing.

Jacob sensed he was lying. *Red, if she dies in your care, or if you're lying to me about how she is, I will raise an army with this thing and hunt for you. I'll make sure to take you down a thousand times before I kill you permanently.*

Then you'd better hurry, Red said reluctantly. *I just checked on her. She's deteriorating quickly. Her breath is shallow and her pulse is slowing. You can't blame me for this one.*

No! They wouldn't make it. Even flying as fast as he could, Cromore was at least ten minutes away.

Jacob! River's terrified voice broke through everything else. *I can't let her die, not again.*

Why is she with you, White? This was a trap, wasn't it!

Red! Listen to me! River pleaded.

River, no!

You can alter her with your blood! You don't need Garion's! Please, please try—

Jacob severed their connection and almost altered in the air.

What have you done? he asked her, doubting his own ears. That hadn't just happened. She hadn't just told Red—and what now? Should he hope that Red tries it and it works on Ivy—or that it doesn't? How many descendants did Red know? Less than a year ago, Jeremy Redmond had been part of a group of descendants who wanted to take down The Bane. El Montgomery, Garion's sister, was part of the same group.

Damn. Damn. Damn.

Garion, he sent out immediately and flew faster, *get in touch with your sister. Find out where she is and go to her.*

I know where she is, Jake. What the hell is it now and why are you heading toward Lewis?

Garion had been searching the Onyx. Obviously, Red was still walking or Garion would have mentioned seeing him. *Keep your eyes on the Onyx*, Jacob suggested. *I think he's going to fly soon.*

Why do you think that? It was Helena, connected through Garion.

Good. It was better to tell them both at the same time.

I think Red can alter descendants, I think we all can and I'm pretty sure Red knows it now.

What the hell are you talking about? Garion demanded. He sounded a bit winded, like he was running...flapping. *I really hope you're joking.*

It wouldn't be funny, his sister chimed in.

I wish I was joking, he told them, *but think about it, Garion. Your existence was foretold. You were born to save Drakkon from extinction. But you weren't meant to do it alone. Your essence has changed us. We're more like you. Gold doesn't kill us and our blood—*

Oh, no, his brother-in-law groaned, understanding what he meant. *Do you know all this for certain? Have you altered River?*

No, Jacob told him. *But Red may have altered Ivy. I'm heading to where he has her now. I'll know shortly.*

He told you where she was, Garion said tightly. *It sounds like a bargain was struck between you and Red. Which one of you gave him the information in exchange for Ivy's life?*

I did, Jacob told him quietly. *She was at the brink of death.*

A long, heavy silence passed and Jacob had the feeling that things had just changed between him and Garion, perhaps his sister, as well. It killed him to think the man who'd saved his life and gave him flight thought he betrayed him. But it was better that Garion be angry with him and not River.

All right, Garion said, retreating. *I'm on my way to Ellie and speaking to her now. If there's anything else, tell Helena.*

There's nothing else. Jacob let them go and continued flying in silence.

Why did you lie to him? River asked silently, having listened in. Her naturally husky cadence was tainted with regret and uncertainty. *You don't always have to protect me.*

But I always will.

You're angry with me. I didn't mean to involve Garion's sister. If anything happens to her, he's never going to forgive you.

Nothing's going to happen to her, he said, praying he was right. *Garion's on his way. She'll be safe with him.*

I panicked, she confessed quietly in his head. *I've never been so afraid in my life. I couldn't bear the thought of losing her again.*

I know, he told her with a long, smoky sigh. He knew why she told Red. He knew she did it for Ivy. He'd been at the point of telling Red himself when Ivy's life was slipping away. In fact, he could have severed the connection quicker, but he hadn't. He'd let Red hear it. He wanted it to work. He wanted Ivy to live, and he wanted to make a Drakkon out of River.

But this is bad, River. If we don't kill Red today and he has this power, there could be ten Drakkon by tomorrow. In a month there could be a hundred.

And what about The Bane? How many of them were left? How many more would be recruited if more Drakkon ruled the sky? How long would it take them to discover the only way to kill the Gold's "children" was to cut off their heads?

Even more reason to kill him then, River said, like a true warrior Red.

You would feel this way still if he saves Ivy?

I haven't forgotten that he killed Noah...and Graham. And if it weren't for him, Ivy wouldn't need saving. She wouldn't be possibly turning into a Drakkon. Oh, my poor father! She shook her head as if the thought of telling him were too much to fathom. *Jacob, do you think it worked. Do you think she's alive?*

We're about to find out. He told her, coming in for a landing behind the small croft house near the harbor. *We're here.*

He changed and swept his robe from River's hands as he let her go. "Stay here," he told her, looking at the small house. What if it worked? What if it hadn't? He wasn't sure he was ready to find out. If it didn't work, Ivy was probably gone. His heart wrenched in its place. "Red could be inside."

He slipped the robe on and took a step forward. River moved in step behind him. He looked over his shoulder and aimed his most menacing stare at her.

She pushed him forward. "Why would he stick around if it worked?"

"What if it didn't and he wants the stone that doesn't exist?"

"He doesn't know how to kill you," she tossed over *her* shoulder, passing him.

He took her by the wrist, springing her back to him. He looked into her eyes, hoping she would see what she meant to him there. "He knows how to kill you though. Stay back, River."

She blinked slowly and breathed, seeing the heart he laid bare. "Okay."

He continued on with her close behind. *Ivy? Ivy?* He reached out, entering the house with caution. She was here. He could smell her.

Jacob?

Her small, soft voice penetrated his thoughts, his blood and bones. His shoulders melted around his neck with an exhalation of breath he felt like he'd been holding for days.

"She's alive," he whispered over his shoulder.

Ivy, are you alone? Jacob asked while River issued forth a hundred questions, clutching his back, ready to start searching.

Yes. Jacob where are you?

They passed the small sitting room without incident and came to a hall with three closed doors, one on each side and one at the end of the hall.

I'm here. He strode to the door at the end of the hall and pushed it open. Behind him, River finally broke free and rushed to the small bed where her sister lay, lifting herself on an elbow.

Jacob smiled watching their reunion. River asked a dozen questions about how her sister felt, to which Ivy responded that she felt better. So much better.

After he checked the rest of the house and deemed it safe, Jacob returned to Ivy. He noticed, as he neared the bed, that her complexion was rosy, her eyes bright blue. Her hair was no longer blue, but it's natural dark, almost black color. There were bruises on her shoulders beneath her torn, dirty sweater and her left eye was a bit swollen. She was healing. She'd been altered. Red had done it.

He kept his smile intact while he spoke to Ivy and sent word to Garion and his sister that it had worked. Red had altered Ivy. He tried not to let their reactions pierce his heart at present. Ivy was alive. She was well.

Red was still walking according to the Onyx, so they didn't know where he was, or if he was turning anyone. They'd found El and were with her. Jacob promised to meet up with them soon.

"What happened?" Ivy asked, sitting up. "Where are we?"

"You don't remember?" Jacob asked.

She shook her head. "I was…home, and then I was here."

She didn't remember being chased down by a dragon. Jacob was glad.

"Where's the man?" she asked next. "I saw him here. The man with one arm from Tarbert."

Jacob moved closer. "Did he speak to you, Ivy? What did he say?" he asked when she nodded.

"I opened my eyes and saw him. His palm was bleeding and he was wrapping it. Mine…" She looked down at her palm and the tender streak running across it caked in blood. "Mine was bleeding, too. He smiled at me and he said, 'Welcome, Daughter, first of my blood'."

Jacob felt sick.

"What did he mean?"

Jacob couldn't help but scowl when River leaped away from the bed and turned away with her hand over her mouth. Was it so horrible that her sister was a Drakkon? So horrible that she could be one, too?

"He…ehm," Jacob began. How does one tell someone that they are now another kind of being? One with ten-inch fangs and scales and wings? "He turned you, Ivy."

"Turned me?" Her eyes filled with tears. How would she handle it? She'd been angry with Jacob for being a Drakkon. "Into what?"

"Drakkon."

For a moment, her eyes took on a haunted, distant look—as if she was remembering something. Something dreadful. "Where's Graham?" she suddenly asked and tried to leave the bed. "The red dragon! It…it…"

River caught her in her arms when she crumbled in a pool of tears. "Graham was running and the dragon flew over him and then…" She looked up at them with eyes stained with tears and sorrow.

Jacob looked away. He liked Graham. He'd liked spending time with him around the table. Graham was a talented musician and had a lot of potential, and he loved Ivy.

I'm going to kill Red, he promised Ivy in her mind. "I have to go," he said out loud. "I have to find him."

"I know where he's going to be," Ivy said, wiping her nose and proving she was every bit of a fighter as her sister. "He wants me to meet him on St. Combs Beach. He told me not to tell you if you asked. I had no idea what he meant at the time. I don't remember anything else until I heard you calling my name."

Jacob's heart thundered. He nearly altered right there. *St. Combs Beach, Garion.*

"Thank you, Ivy." He leaned down and cupped her head in his hands. *I'll come back and teach you about Drakkon. We'll fly together.* He pulled a smile from her and kissed her forehead.

When he stepped back, River was there. Hell, it was difficult looking at her and knowing he had to leave. From the moment he'd arrived in Harris, he'd made it his purpose to protect her. Now he knew why. She was his life mate. If he lost her, he would lose it all.

"You need to stay with your sister," he said, taking her hand and holding it between them.

Her big, beautiful eyes filled with tears and she nodded, giving in. She took his hand and led him back out of the house. "Don't get killed," she said, turning to him with the wind blowing her hair across her eyes. "We have things to talk about."

Right. Like her becoming a Drakkon. He didn't need Garion to agree, though he'd prefer his family's blessing. But he did need River to agree. Would she? His mouth went dry and he swiped his tongue over his bottom lip. Did she still want him to leave when this was over?

"For a moment up there," she told him, hugging herself instead of him, "I thought you were going to let me fall."

No, no, he never wanted her to think that. He closed the gap between them and took her in his arms. "River, I'll never fly again after today if you believe that."

"I'd never ask you to give that up for me," she told him, her breath warm against his lips.

He kissed her. There were a thousand questions he wanted to ask her, a thousand reassurances he longed to hear her say. But he kissed her because she was his and he treasured her above all else, not because it was a Drakkon instinct, but because she'd taken up the broken pieces and made him whole, finally complete. He wasn't leaving. He wasn't letting her go, and he showed her with his lips, his tongue, his hands along her back, drawing her in closer as he deepened his kiss.

When he finally withdrew, he stared into her eyes. He spoke softly and slowly, running his fingers down a lock of her hair. "I want to spend eternity with you, River."

She veiled her eyes from his. His heart sank. He'd never considered that she wouldn't want to change. Why would she? Drakkon ruined her life and killed her friends.

He turned away without another word, slipped his robe off, and flew away.

CHAPTER TWENTY-THREE

J ACOB PIERCED THE clouds and soared low over The Minch, a strait separating the Inner Hebrides from the Outer, and then swung around the Orkney Islands to the North Sea and the coast. He didn't care who saw him flying. They'd never have proof, a fact they'd learned from Ivy.

He was happy Red's blood had been able to alter River's sister. He'd do everything he could to stop Red from turning anyone else, and mend what he'd broken with Garion. He'd just discovered that belonging to a family had been his heart's desire. He wasn't about to start losing members of it now.

He tried to keep his thoughts on Red, but River seeped into every corner of his mind like a mist, dousing every fire inside him but the one that burned for her. If he'd lost her, he'd win her back. If she chose not to be transformed, he would live each day with her until it was their last, making her happy, helping her make her dreams come true.

Where are you guys? He reached out to Helena and Garion after surveying the sky and the coastline of St. Combs Beach.

I just passed the Isle of May, his brother-in-law informed him. *Helena stayed in Arran with Ellie. Anything from Red?*

Garion's brevity fell upon him like a sharpened sword. *No, nothing,* Jacob told him. *Listen Garion—*

I'd really rather not, his brother-in-law cut him off. *We need to stay focused.*

We will, Jacob said. *This will only take a second. Ivy, who had not been dead as we believed, was taking her last breaths. River was listening to her sister die. I was losing them both. My family...my treasure. I can only hope you would do the same for Helena.*

It was quiet for a little while. There was nothing more to say. Garion either understood and could forgive him, or not.

Jacob landed on the sandy shore and looked around. He saw a small stone shed with a square hole for a window a short way down the coastline. He lifted his spiked head to sniff the air.

Jake, Garion's voice sounded in his ears, quiet, softer. *I would.*

Yeah, Jacob answered happily, not really surprised but glad to hear it. Things would be okay with Garion.

He stuck his head inside the dark shed and smelled the place. He picked up a slight trace of urine and something else, possibly Drakkon.

Jake! Garion's voice rumbled through his head. *He's flying! He's heading toward St. Combs Beach. I'll be there in five minutes!*

Jacob altered and stepped into the shed. He bent to his knees and looked outside the square window at the sky. He saw nothing but clouds for a moment or two and was about to turn his attention to a large duffle bag in the shadows. Something reddish-gold flashed against the sun.

He's here, Jacob sent to Garion.

Crimson wings painted the sky as the Red dipped below the clouds and flew toward the shore a half-mile north.

Jacob wasted no time but leaped from the window and into the sky. He spread his wings, momentarily blocking the shed from the sun, and then set off after Red. He hoped to catch him as he landed and altered. One bite was all it would take. Though the thought sickened him and pulled him toward humanity, he resisted. Right now, he had to be Drakkon.

He spotted his prey landing along a rocky incline. The air changed and the Red shimmered into dust, leaving a man behind.

Triumph brought a snarl to Jacob's mouth. He pulled his wings in close and dove toward Red, his jaws spreading wide. This was for Graham and Noah, and for all the pain he caused River.

Jeremy turned just several seconds before he lost his head. Eyes wide with surprise and horror, he threw himself to the ground, rolled, and came back up breathing fire.

Damn it, Jacob thought, diving into the water to avoid the flames. When Red's fire was gone, Jacob came back up and met him in the air. He snapped his twelve-inch fangs at Red's face. He caught the Drakkon's snout and bit down but he couldn't pierce Drakkon's scales. It was their armor, only penetrable with pure gold.

Red swished his spaded tail and nearly hit Jacob in the ribs. They separated in the sky and then flew at each other again.

Jacob recalled what Garion had told him. If Red was Drakkon they should forget his head and go for his wings. Take him down. Kill him while he altered. Jacob tried to swing his neck around and bite but Red's clicking fangs near his eyes stopped him.

Having both his arms gave Jacob the advantage. He swiped his razor sharp claws at Red's face then used the power in his thighs to kick Red in the belly. Blood-red wings flapped unevenly while Red tumbled backward.

Jacob sensed Garion close and turned to see him almost upon them. Red had no time to fly out of the way when Garion smashed into him, knocking him twenty feet away.

Red altered into a man for just a second as pain coursed through him. His scales returned almost instantly and he held back Jacob's teeth with a kick that sent Jacob sprawling.

Garion attacked, biting at Red's wings, but Red fought furiously and got away. He flew for the ocean and dove deep within its churning waves. Garion followed, disappearing beneath the surface.

Jacob waited in the air. Red would have to come up at some point. Drakkon weren't designed to breathe under water for longer than fifteen minutes. He'd be hot on Red's tail when he came up.

Sooner than he expected, Red broke through the surface like an arrow shot from some fiery pit and landed where Jacob had come in.

Jacob took off after him and heard Garion erupt from the sea next. *He's going for the shed. I saw a bag in the corner.*

A weapon maybe, Garion said, passing him with a mighty flap. *Be careful.*

Right. Why didn't we bring any? Jacob asked as Red reached the shed moments before them, altered, and disappeared into the enclosure.

Garion didn't wait to see what he was up to inside. He flew into the stone walls with the weight of his body, protected by his armor. He clutched the rooftop with his mighty talons and tore the stones away.

Red leaped out of the rubble with a shotgun pointed up. He shot the first thing he saw.

Jacob felt the sting of the gold bullet penetrating his scales, his muscle and deeper. He was turning. He tried to hold on until the fall wouldn't hurt him further. He wouldn't die, but he'd be helpless for the next three minutes while his body healed.

He heard another shot and watched Garion go down in the next instant.

This wasn't happening. They couldn't lose him. They couldn't waste time healing while he was out there altering descendants.

When Red tossed the shotgun away and altered back to Drakkon, Jacob realized they might not get the chance to hunt him again. Red could eat them—

Was that an Aqua he saw flying over Red's scaly shoulder? What the hell? Who the hell was it?

Jacob.

River. His heart raced, pumping blood from his wounds. He had to stay conscious. *Is that...Ivy?* he asked, hoping he was dreaming. Ivy couldn't fight Red! *Where are you?*

Hitching a ride.

Oh no. Hell, no! She was on Ivy's back? Was she crazy? *River, what the hell—*

How do I cut off its head? River asked over him. *I have the sword Garion left at the house. Hurry!*

Ivy was getting closer to Red. Red was getting closer to him and Garion. Any minute now, Red would sense her and turn his head to see her, or open his mouth and have the two pesky men for lunch.

He tried to change, but this time it wasn't up to his will. He didn't have three minutes.

His wings! He told her quickly. *Ivy needs to bite off his damn wing. Then, when he falls, you cut off his head. But River—*

He didn't want her to be the one to do it. What she was doing was madness—riding a Drakkon to fight another Drakkon when she was mortal! He should have altered her, then if Red—

Garion, Red said, pressing his nose to Garion's bloody chest. *I wish things could have been different between us. But you were selfish. You wanted all this power for yourself. Well, guess what? I don't need your blood anymore.*

I know, Garion replied.

Jacob was glad his eyes were open so he could witness the perplexed arch of Red's spiked brow an instant before the Aqua swooped in and sank her fangs into the base of his leathery wing. She managed to avoid his swinging tail and didn't let go until she tore it from his shoulder.

Jacob's heart leaped at the sight of Red falling to the ground, a Drakkon stripped of flight, a man defeated.

He sat up a moment later in dreadful anticipation when Ivy landed near him and River jumped from the nook between her sister's shoulders. "I told you I'd kill you," she said while her sister held him down with her claw and she lifted the sword high above her head. "This is how it's done."

She brought the blade down with all her strength, her flaming hair swinging around her face, and swiped off his head in one blow.

Jacob wanted to lie back and breathe with such relief it made him lightheaded. But he couldn't take his eyes off her. His warrior life mate. She'd be a formidable Drakkon. Taking her to the stars in the ancient dance of the beast was almost too tempting to fight off.

She turned to look at him and the bloody holes in his belly. She knew he'd live but he knew it looked bad when her eyes filled with tears. *I almost lost you.* She dropped the sword and went to her Drakkon sister, who sat on her haunches, waiting for her. With a shrug of Ivy's scaled shoulders, two robes fell to the ground. River picked them up and tossed one to Garion and then went to Jacob.

She covered his lap with the robe and then went to her knees before him and stared into his level, loving gaze. "When I saw you lying here…" She stopped and ran her shimmering gaze over his belly, "all I could think was how glad I was that you hadn't turned me. I imagined an eternity without you…and I'd rather die now."

He looked into her eyes and struggled to keep his disappointment concealed from her. Was this it then? She didn't want to be Drakkon? He closed his eyes and lay back down, letting his body recover. His heart never would when he lost her. "I understand."

She leaned down over him and whispered close to his mouth. "So do I, that's why I want you to turn me." She offered him an intimate smile when he opened his eyes and looked into hers. "Later."

LATER COULDN'T COME soon enough for Jacob.

Still, he had to admit that sitting at the dinner table in River's kitchen, crammed as they were with the addition of Garion's sister, El, was the only thing he'd rather be doing if he couldn't be alone with River.

Garion didn't argue when Jacob told him he was going to alter River. *Your sister doesn't want you to ever be alone again. Neither do I*, he told Jacob instead.

Things between them were restored. Jacob was glad. He loved the quiet Gold. He sent a silent thank you to his sister, knowing it was she who'd convinced her husband to accept it. The sky was going to change. It was the purpose for which Garion had been born.

They'd broken the news gently to Hagan Wray that Ivy was a Drakkon and River had chosen to be one, as well. He took it better than they had expected.

"I've lived with one in my head for the last twenty-two years, children," he told them. "I knew it was real. None could convince me otherwise. It wasn't the dragon that hurt me though. It was everyone else. Now, a dragon—Drakkon," he corrected with a smile aimed at

Jacob, "has vindicated me before my accusers and brought a truth to the light which I should not have kept to myself." He turned his warm gaze on his daughters. "I've always known my girls were strong and fierce, even if they didn't always know it. If they want to be Drakkons, I have no problems with it." He made a toast to Graham and Noah that made Ivy cry. River was there to comfort her.

"Yes," Garion's sister, El, sighed, aiming her large, luminous, turquoise gaze at her brother. "Not all of us will live forever."

Garion rolled his eyes and continued eating.

"When are you going to turn me, Garion?" El slapped her hand down on the table, frustrated with him yet again. "I don't need your blood anymore," she threw at him and turned to Jacob.

He smiled. He liked El. She was strong-minded and almost as arrogant as her father. "Don't look at me," he told her.

She turned to Helena, who also refused. They were loyal to Garion's wishes.

Finally, she looked at Ivy and smiled.

"If Garion says no, then it's no," Ivy told her.

Garion smiled at her from across the table.

El dropped her chin into her hand and sighed. "I should have let Jeremy find me."

"Why didn't you?" Garion asked and handed a piece of salmon to Carina in his lap.

"Because I didn't want that creep to alter me. I want my brother to do it. How can you continue to deny me when everyone around me is Drakkon? I swear, I feel like the least important person in your life."

Garion stopped eating. Jacob sensed his brother-in-law's resolve faltering and smiled. As far as important people in Garion's life went, it was Helena and then El and then everyone after them. El knew it but she also knew how to play with his emotions.

"I'll think about it," he finally gave in.

She nearly flew out of her chair and flung her arms around his neck.

Caught up in their warm affection, Jacob pulled River closer. He still couldn't believe what she'd done today. She'd saved him and Garion from a Drakkon. She'd saved everyone else, too. She could have lost her life and yet, she did it. She radiated with confidence. The longing he'd seen in her eyes when they had first met in the shop was gone. Was he the fulfillment of her longing, as she was to him? Or did it have to do with what straightened her shoulders and made her look ready for anything?

It's you, my love, she answered his thoughts, now privy to them whenever she chose to be. *You are what I've longed for. You're my closest, closest friend who knows me better than I know myself. The man I love and adore above all else. I want to spend eternity with you.*

His heart felt as if it burst into stardust and then formed again. As crazy as it was, he had Red to thank for bringing them together. Though, he wasn't certain he could have stayed away to begin with. She'd shined like a light that first day on the crags, and only grew brighter from then on, until all he could see was her.

Her scent enveloped him now. Desire made his blood burn. He wanted to turn her. He ached to do it. He was tired of waiting.

He gently touched her thoughts. *Let's go take a walk.*

What will we tell—

Jacob stood up from his chair, bringing River with him. "We're going for a walk."

"To...ehm..." River paused to smile at her father while Jacob tugged her hand, "discuss our...wedding."

Right? She turned to him and asked silently when he finally stopped pulling and stared at her.

Right, he agreed, letting his smile spread over her.

Everyone jumped out of their chairs to congratulate them even though almost everyone there knew they were life mates. Jacob had to fend his sister off three separate times when she tried to haul River away to discuss the wedding plans.

"Oh! You should do it at my parents'!" El suggested. "River, you'd love it. They live in a beautiful castle in—"

"Or, we can plan something in Italy!" Helena wouldn't give up.

"We'll decide and let you know," Jacob told them and blocked out the chirping voices of his sister, El, and Ivy. Poor Garion and Hagan he thought as he hurried out of the house with his love, ready to see her in her full, radiant glory.

DARKNESS SETTLED OVER Camasunary Bay. The sound of waves rolling in along the shore blended with Jacob's short, shallow breaths against her ear, her chin, her lips.

They lay naked beneath the stars, entangled in each other's arms and legs, touching, kissing, laughing as their passion swelled.

River gazed into his eyes while she made love to him. They spoke to her, revealing his heart and how deeply he loved her, how precious and beautiful she was to him.

"I wonder how I lived before I met you," Jacob's heavy, languid voice fell over her ears like mesmerizing music. "You've awakened me, just as you did that early winter morning. Now, I feel everything." He quirked his mouth at her and thrust again.

"You were extraordinary today," he told her on a low growl, moving his fingers through her hair, over her features. He licked the seam of her mouth then bit her lip and drove himself into her again. "Fearsome and sexy as hell."

Every part of her screamed out for release. He commanded her muscles to respond to his slow, salacious movements. She clenched him tighter, rubbed herself against him as he sank deep and then retreated. She smiled and spread her tongue where he'd licked her mouth. He dipped his face and bit her chin. She pulled his hair loose from its clip and watched his silky locks fall around his face. "Tell me how I won your heart," she whispered against his lips and lifted her legs high around him.

"It was your strength to battle fear and win." He kissed her bottom lip, pressing his hips to hers. "Your courage to stand before a Drakkon and offer it a deal." He smiled into her eyes and shifted his weight. She gasped, close to release. "It was the music you played to my soul that made the stars lose their glimmer." He ran his tongue down her throat and whispered over her goose-fleshed skin. "It was the look of you, the scent of you, the way you sound to my ears and in my head. I'm never letting you go."

After her teary climax in his arms, he held her close and whispered against her ear. "Are you ready to make this eternal, my love?"

She nodded, staying where she was while he sat up. She was ready to spend forever with him...and her sister. There was no denying it, she and Drakkon were written in the stars. He altered and peered down at her from his enormous eyes. *Don't be afraid,* he sent her, holding up a razor sharp claw. *It will heal quickly.* He made a small slice above her left rib then cut himself on his right side and altered back into a man. He moved toward her and gathered her up to press their wounds together.

She didn't feel anything but their hearts beating together, then she became aware that they were in perfect sync. Her vision also changed and Jacob's fine chiseled features became clearer. "You smell good," she told him and he smiled and kissed her while their blood mixed.

You're Drakkon, he let her know. *Just a moment to change your life forever.*

You changed my life forever the moment I first saw you...both times, she assured him, reaching up to touch his face.

He kissed her fingers. "How do you feel?"

"Good." She smiled. "Very good as a matter of fact."

"Are you ready to fly?"

She was ready to fly. She wasn't ready to turn. "I think so."

He stood up and sent thoughts to her of flying with him, dancing to the stars with him. He altered in a flash of glimmering light and stepped back, beckoning her to the sky.

Her heart hammered in her chest at the thought of being Drakkon, of having scales and breathing fire. There wasn't any pain, just a sense of coming apart. She almost altered twice but returned to her human form.

You can fly, my love. Go all the places you've dreamed of going.

I dream of being in your arms, she told him and burst forth in a flurry of scarlet wings tipped in aqua and traces of gold. She flapped wildly at first, lifting her ruby talons off the ground. She had talons! Wings! She was gigantic. Smaller than Jacob but not by much.

I knew you'd be a beautiful Drakkon, Jacob sent, flying to her and meeting her in the air. *You take my breath away. My life mate. My treasure beyond all comprehension.* They flew together, untethered to the cares of the world below. She sang to him, filling them both with the boundless joy of freedom. When her thoughts of making love to him again made her begin to shift and alter, he took her in his mighty, scaled arms. *Take me as Drakkon and let me take you to the stars.*

Her Drakkon form returned almost instantly and she snapped her great fangs at him when he coiled his tail around hers. He held her still for a moment while he penetrated her. She filled the sky with a loud, languid groan. The stars answered with music that made her dance.

Entwined in their limbs and tails, they rode the wind and twirled toward the stars in a vortex of iridescent light, four softly flapping wings, and the purity of love that brought them higher than either of them had ever dared to dream.

EPILOGUE

The Northern borders of England
One month later

JACOB HAD TRAVELED to a number of beautiful places in the last month. His and River's lives had become a whirlwind. They were married on a beach in Tahiti then flew—by plane—to New York to sign River with an A&R rep. After that, Jacob whisked her off to L.A. to meet with *Everbound* while they were touring.

But nothing compared in beauty to the magnificent castle belonging to Marcus and Samantha Aquara up ahead. It looked like something straight out of medieval days. Jacob knew Marcus had put a small chunk of his fortune into the castle. If this was paid for with a small chunk, how much did he have?

Perched on the windswept moors, alone under the charcoal sky, it boasted two round, crenellated keeps between the main building and high, stone battlements. They drove over a sturdy twenty-first century drawbridge and entered the outer bailey, surrounded by a low stone wall. There were gardens throughout the bailey where every kind of summer flower bloomed.

"This is it," he said, shutting off the ignition to the Mercedes in front of double massive wooded doors with wrought iron fixtures.

"Wait," Hagan Wray said from the backseat where he sat with Ivy. "What if he remembers me? What if he doesn't want any witnesses?"

Jacob didn't know Marcus all that well. Could Mr. Wray's fears be correct? Maybe Marcus wouldn't like to be reminded of his days as Drakkon. "Nah. It's his birthday. He's like a thousand or something. I'm sure the last thing on his mind is picking fights."

Garion greeted them at the doors and showed them inside. The interior of the castle was even grander than the outside. Painted walls, wide, paneled windows, and electricity gave it a more modern feel, while paintings of landscapes and skyscapes lined the softly lit halls. Ornately carved banisters led to a second and third floor. Soft music wafted outward from the grand solar, where Garion led them next.

"I love this place," River echoed his thoughts as they stepped inside.

Tapestries sewn in warm hues hung from walls bathed in the soft ambience of a wood and wrought iron chandelier and a large hearth fire. Large, overstuffed sofas and chairs upholstered in brown leather and teal and gold throws beckoned Jacob to sit.

A woman stood off by the doorway of an adjacent room. Jacob recognized her from the island. Samantha Montgomery, bestselling romance author and life mate of Marrkiya the Aqua. She was a petite woman with beautiful dark eyes and short, pixyish hair. She took a step in his direction, but Helena, coming in from the adjacent room, saw him and hurried past her.

"They have a ballroom!" she uttered, giving her husband a nervous look. "They're not going to want us to dance, are they?"

"No, it's for them," Garion soothed. "They dance."

Helena cocked her brow. "Alone? In a ballroom?"

"My father likes to do things big."

"Did you tell them?" Helena asked her husband next, forgetting the ballroom.

"Tell us what?" Jacob asked looking at them both.

No one had time to answer when a man's voice nearly brought the walls down around them.

"You can't make it? I haven't seen you since winter!"

"Ehm…" Hagan Wray swallowed as Marcus stormed into the solar. 6'4" of pure, brawny muscle. "He doesn't look a thousand years old." He started to turn around the same way he'd come in, but River and Ivy stopped him.

"You're not afraid of him, are you?" Garion asked him. "He knows about you. He wants to meet you. Come."

Hagan didn't move. Neither did River or her sister. Marcus was a formidable man, especially when he was shouting.

"Ellie?" he spoke into the phone then looked up with such a dark scowl, everyone looking at him took a step back. "She's not coming. She has to work."

His wife hurried to his side and his anger dissolved into a sigh.

"Dad," Garion said, pulling them forward. "Your guests are here."

Marcus set down his phone and went to them with Samantha under his arm. He greeted Jacob with a warm, tight embrace, a pat on the back, and a soft slap to the cheek. "You should have had your wedding here."

"I didn't want to impose."

"Nonsense, you're family now, Jake."

Jacob smiled, feeling like a fool for feeling choked up.

Marcus moved on to River and Ivy next. He stared at River's eyes and Ivy's soft blue bob. "I would have known you were both Aqua the instant I saw you." He shifted his eyes, a deeper shade of cerulean than theirs, to Garion and Jacob and shook his head. "Pitiful that you didn't know."

He slipped his cool gaze to River's father and looked him over until Hagan began to squirm. "I'm told you saw me flying."

Hagan Wray was pale and Jacob was almost sure he could hear his heart beating as he nodded. "Yes. I did. You were…incredible."

"Yes," Marcus agreed. "I was. Come," he tossed his arm around Hagan's shoulder. "Tell me about it."

"So," Jacob turned to his sister. "What haven't you told us?"

"I'm pregnant," she announced, beaming. Her husband looked a bit more worried, but happy.

"But how?" Jacob asked him. "We were both cut."

Garion shrugged his broad shoulders. "I don't know, but Helena's pregnant. River might be, too."

Jacob was glad. There was nothing more he wanted in the world than his own family. He slipped his gaze to his beautiful wife and smiled with her.

"She's here," Garion's voice broke his thoughts of possibly being a father.

"Dad," he called out to Marcus. "Come with me outside for a minute."

The skies were quiet as everyone followed them out. Marcus waited, instinctively looking up. He narrowed his deep aqua eyes on something in the distant clouds. He realized after a moment what it was. A Drakkon. An Aqua.

"Is that…" he asked with pulled breath.

"Ellie," Garion told him as she flew closer.

There were tears in Marcus' eyes while he watched his daughter in the sky. "She's beautiful."

Jacob agreed, staring into his wife's eyes. He loved her. He loved being a part of this big family of theirs.

Priceless treasures.

ABOUT THE AUTHOR

Paula Quinn is a New York Times bestselling author and a sappy romantic moved by music, beautiful words, and the sight of a really nice pen. She lives in New York with her three beautiful children, six over-protective chihuahuas, and three adorable parrots. She loves to read romance and science fiction and has been writing since she was eleven. She's a faithful believer in God and thanks Him daily for all the blessings in her life.

FB:
facebook.com/PaulaQuinnAuthor

Twitter:
@Paula_Quinn

Website:
pa0854.wixsite.com/paulaquinn

CPSIA information can be obtained
at www.ICGtesting.com
Printed in the USA
LVHW05s0625200718
584415LV00009B/171/P

JUL 2 6 2018